Just a Cowboy's Happy Ever After

Flyboys of Sweet Briar Ranch in North Dakota
Book Thirteen
Jessie Gussman

Published By: Jessie Gussman

Contents

Acknowledgments

Cover art by Julia Gussman
Editing by Heather Hayden
Narration by Jay Dyess
Author Services by CE Author Assistant

Listen to a FREE professionally performed and produced audio-book version of this title on Youtube. Search for "Say With Jay" to browse all available FREE Dyess/Gussman audiobooks.

Chapter 1

"Go ahead and use the basement door. You can take it right to the kitchen and set it on the counter. That insulated wrap should keep it warm."

Lark Stryker directed Heavenne, one of the girls who lived with her, toward the church basement to keep her out of the way of the funeral goers, who were mostly going in the front door, the one leading directly to the sanctuary.

"Should I follow her?" Katrina asked, looking to Lark for guidance.

Heavenne and Katrina were both fifteen and had both been sent to Lark's care by their parents. Neither of them were terribly bad girls, they just needed someone to take an interest in them and give them a little bit of direction and attention.

Possibly disconnecting them from social media had been something else they'd needed.

"Yes. Yours should be able to go on the counter as well, but make sure you put it where the cold dishes are located."

If it weren't for the girls in her care, four of them right now—aside from Heavenne and Katrina, she had Kay and Erin, who were both thirteen—she wouldn't be here.

Taking a breath, she directed Kay to take the cake that she had made and follow the other two.

"Do you think anybody's going to like this?" Erin asked, biting her lip as she held the 7 layer magic bars she'd made.

It was the first time she'd made anything to take outside their home, which was a huge accomplishment for her, since when she first came to Lark's house, she hadn't wanted to even set foot in the kitchen.

"I think they're going to love it. Those bars are a favorite everywhere. And you did a great job on them," Lark said, putting a hand on Erin's shoulder and giving her a side hug.

Erin laid her head on Lark's arm just for a moment before she straightened. She was at that age where she was still so much a little girl but starting to become a woman as well.

Snuggling into another adult, one who was acting as a mother figure, wasn't exactly a mature thing for her to do.

Still, as long as she would allow hugs and other displays of affection, Lark would hand them out. Her mom had been excellent at that. Lark had never wondered whether her mom loved her. She said so, but she also showed them. Not just with hugs and the way she stroked Lark's hair or kissed her forehead, but because of the service that she did. Her mom would do anything to help her children, and Lark had that full confidence riding behind her all of her life.

There was no doubt in her mind that her mom thought she was amazing and she loved her.

Until she had gotten a little older, she was thirty-five now, she hadn't realized how valuable a feeling like that was. And the girls who came to her house typically didn't have that. Not about their mom and, more often, not about their dad either.

Most of the time, they weren't sure whether either one of their parents cared for them at all. They felt unwanted, like they were a mistake, in the way, an annoyance.

Sometimes they went out of their way to be those things, just because they didn't know how to be anything else. Or because the idea of having love and affection was too unusual and scary.

Sometimes dealing with girls like that was exhausting, but Lark relished it, along with her work as a veterinarian.

It kept her mind off other things.

Like Jeb Malone. The man who was burying his wife today.

Steeling herself, pushing her shoulders back just a little, and grabbing the crockpot with the sliced ham in it, she balanced it on her hip while she hit the button to shut the back of her car.

Again she thought, if it were just her, she wouldn't be here, but the girls who lived with her needed to see her serving and needed to learn to serve the community. Part of that was helping to provide food for the funerals that were held at the Sweet Water church.

Lark would have liked to back out of this one. Just because she'd managed to avoid Jeb ever since she'd graduated from vet school and started her own practice.

He never called her, despite owning a large dairy, and that was just fine by her.

Once upon a time, she thought she would marry him.

He refused. She might have fallen into a deep depression, but someone, she wasn't sure who, had offered to pay for vet school.

She corresponded with her benefactor all through college and vet school, continuing even after she graduated. Which was another part of why she was at the funeral today—her benefactor, after years of refusing her offers to meet so she could thank him in person, finally asked to meet her. She'd agreed immediately, of course, and they'd set up a time that happened to be after the funeral and meal, meeting at the big oak tree behind the old white church in Sweet Water.

She couldn't think of that meeting without being a little nervous. The man, whoever he was, had paid for all her schooling, had bought her farm, and had provided a way for her to help the girls who lived with her.

Having the girls was her way of giving back to the community, since her benefactor had invested so heavily into her.

If it hadn't been for him, his encouraging letters, his monetary support, she wasn't sure where she would be today.

Regardless, for the immediate future, she figured it was probably too much for her to hope to make it through the rest of the day without seeing Jeb, so she steeled herself and tried to remind herself that she was a mature, grown woman, and she could handle seeing an old crush. Even one who had so brutally rejected her.

And then married someone else.

"Lark! Sweetheart. Let me help you with that." Her mother hurried toward Lark.

"Mom, I've got it. You can get the door though," Lark said with a smile at her mom who, despite her advancing years, still walked with a spring in her step, even if it had gotten a little slower over the years.

"Where's Howard?" she asked about the man her mom had married several years ago. It was about time too, since Lark's dad had died when she was just a little girl. Her mom had raised all eight of her children on her own.

"He carried my stuff in, and I just came back out to the car for these." Her mom held up napkins.

That didn't really make Lark feel bad, even though the thought crossed her mind that if she had a husband, he would be carrying the crockpot for her most likely. Although, she knew there were women who were married to men who didn't think to do anything kind for their wives.

"I know a funeral isn't a great place to meet people, but there's someone I want you to meet."

"Mom." Lark leaned her head to the side and gave her mom a look that she hadn't used in a really long time.

It used to be when she was in college, and especially vet school, her mom would ask almost every other weekend whether she had found someone.

She never told her mom that she was still pining over Jeb. It seemed like when she gave her heart, she gave it completely and couldn't take it back, even if it was thrown at her. Or maybe she accidentally ducked when he threw it, and it missed her, landing somewhere where she couldn't find it.

She almost laughed at the whimsical idea. She just...wasn't someone who fell in love easily, she supposed.

"I know. I learned a long time ago that it's just best for me to keep my mouth shut and to stay out of my children's business. But this is a special case. Please believe me when I say that I have your best interest at heart."

"I know you do, Mom. You always have. I appreciate it."

She'd let her mom introduce her to whoever she wanted to, just because her mom had earned that right, over and over and over again. She couldn't imagine having a better mother.

But she wasn't the slightest bit interested in meeting someone. Not now, not ever. She'd put everything on the line when she'd fallen for Jeb, and she supposed there were some things a person just couldn't recover from.

"All right. You take these things in, set them on the counter, and you come on back out here."

"Mom, it's a funeral."

"I know. I know. But I'm telling you, this is the chance of a lifetime. And I know that that's a pretty big statement, but just listen, it's like this: my husband worked with his dad. They grew up together. His dad decided to not exactly go off-grid, but to be a little more self-sufficient, just raise his kids and his family on a farm. They ended up having six boys and six girls."

"Twelve kids?" It was unusual to find anyone with eight children in their family, the way she had with her siblings. It just wasn't done anymore. Unless a person was Amish or Mennonite.

"Yes. Twelve kids. They actually have more than we do."

"That's rare."

"I told you." Her mom smiled, and it wasn't hard to hear the barely contained excitement in her voice. "So, you have that in common with him. And the entire family has just relocated to a ranch just outside of Sweet Water. We have the Sweet Water Ranch, of course. And we have Sweet Briar Ranch, plus we have the Coleman trucking company and the Baldwin sale barn. Now, we have the Sweet View ranch, and all twelve siblings are going to be living on it."

"All twelve?"

"Apparently the parents were killed in a car accident. It happened right by the ranch that they were living on down in Wyoming, and the siblings decided they wanted a fresh start."

Lark's mom went on about the man she wanted Lark to meet. Lark couldn't disagree that he sounded like a really nice guy. Successful. A family man. Someone who was loyal to his siblings, even when he might be better off leaving and doing something on his own.

Those were all things she admired in someone. But since she'd been fifteen, there had only been one man for her and she hadn't really been able to look at anyone else.

She didn't think, despite the twenty years that had gone by, that anything had changed.

"Oh! There he is!" her mom said, grabbing her arm and practically dragging her along.

It was so out of character for her mom. Normally, she just sat back and allowed things to happen. She prayed a lot but didn't do a lot of manipulation in her children's lives.

Because it was so unusual, Lark felt like she had to go along with it. Her mom asked for so very little, after giving her so very much.

"Ezra!" her mom called, making Lark feel like she was twelve and giving her the strongest desire to bury her head in the sand. "Ezra! This is my daughter who I was telling you about!"

"Mom. I'll follow you. You don't have to drag me like I'm a sled," Lark gritted out between teeth that were clamped together.

Her mom slowed, looking at where she held tight to Lark's arm. She loosened her fingers and said softly, "I'm sorry. I just...just want you to be happy." Her mom turned and gave Lark the most tender look. It made Lark feel guilty for even saying anything.

"Mom. I am happy."

"But you need to be married. You need a mate. A partner. Someone who's going to support you and be with you, who will love you the way you deserve to be loved."

"Mom. I don't need that. I have Jesus."

Her mom's mouth opened, then closed, then opened again. Finally, she closed it, pressed her lips together, and shook her head. "How can I argue with that?"

"You're the one who taught it to me. Of course God wants us to get married. He didn't create us to be alone, but He also wanted us to be able to depend on Jesus and say that He is enough."

"I know."

"Did you call me?" a man's voice said, causing both Lark and her mother to turn.

It was a voice that spoke of responsibility and hard work and loyalty and character.

Lark couldn't fault her mom. If she were looking for a man, this man would be an excellent choice. How he managed to remain unmarried at his age was anyone's guess.

Maybe he was divorced, but he didn't look like the kind of man who would leave his wife, and a woman would have to be crazy to walk away from a man with character like that.

But sometimes people made huge mistakes and never recovered from them.

"I called you. I want you to meet my daughter, Lark. She's the veterinarian around Sweet Water."

"Along with my partner," Lark added, because she couldn't take all the credit.

"Lark. I've heard a lot about you. It's good to meet you," the man said, holding out his hand. "I'm Ezra."

The man's handshake was firm, his hand dry and rough with calluses.

He would be a good man to have as a friend and definitely a great asset to the community, but Lark couldn't say that she was the slightest bit interested in being anything more than friends with him.

She supposed young love died hard for most people, but for her, it seemed to be like a bad weed that just wouldn't die.

"It's good to meet you. I'm Lark. I heard you're moving in with your entire family."

"Yeah. We needed a change. We're relocating, all of us together. I know it's a little bit weird, but anyone with twelve kids in their family these days is going to be a little weird."

Lark laughed and agreed with that assessment.

They chatted for a bit, with Lark trying to put the effort in that her mom expected of her.

She might be thirty-five, but she still wanted to please her mom. She didn't figure that would ever change.

Still, as the parking lot got more crowded, she finally said, "I better go. My girls are helping with the meal, and I need to make sure that everything's happening the way it should. Are you still good to take them home?" she asked her mom. She'd agreed to take the girls so Lark could go to her meeting at the old church.

Her mom nodded, but Lark could see the disappointment in her mother's face, and it cut at her heart.

She didn't want to disappoint her mom. Actually, she knew that her mom was pleased with whatever she did. The problem was, she worried about Lark.

Lark couldn't blame her. Any of the girls that had been in her care, no matter for how short of a time, she wanted them to succeed in life, to be happy.

That's all her mom wanted for her, and Lark couldn't fault her.

The problem was, there would never be anyone for her but Jeb.

Lark went into the kitchen, chatting with the ladies who were there and praising her girls for the good job that they had been doing.

The funeral was about to start, and while Lark wished she could stay in the basement, she herded her girls together, and they went up the stairs. The girls saw some other teens sitting in the middle of the rows of pews, and Lark nodded when they asked if they could sit in the pew directly behind them, which was half-empty.

They walked away, and Lark stopped for just a moment, taking a breath and looking at the man she hadn't seen for years.

He stood at the front of the church, his profile to her, facing the head of the coffin. It was still open.

She supposed they'd shut it before the funeral began, but for now, people milled about, standing at the coffin, talking to the man in low voices, although he didn't have much to say.

Jeb never really did talk much. She could tell within the first thirty seconds that hadn't changed at all.

It made her smile. She talked enough for both of them. At least she had when she was younger. She supposed she didn't talk quite as much now as she did then.

Still, she always thought that was a good balance in their personalities. He didn't talk, she did. He wasn't very social, she was. He was very serious, she couldn't help but be happy and smiling about pretty much everything.

There were a lot of opposites in their personalities, but their core values were exactly the same.

She swallowed. Jeb saw things differently about their relationship, though. It was one of the few things that they disagreed on.

Of course, she didn't know they disagreed on it until she proposed to him.

His wife lay in front of him. Lark could see the thatch of silver hair, the hands folded over the chest, lying still above the blanket tucked around the body.

Her heart cramped, seizing and feeling like it stopped in her chest before it started beating hard and slow, big, painful thumps.

It was hard to pull breath into her lungs, but she straightened her back to provide more room, until she could feel her lungs fill and blow out slowly against the pain.

She could do this. She could walk up the aisle, sit down, and attend this funeral. Even while Jeb sat just feet away from her.

She could go back downstairs and serve the meal, chatting and smiling at people, being kind, even if that included serving Jeb.

Somehow, she doubted he'd come through the line.

Still, if he did, she could handle it.

What she wasn't sure she could handle was having Jeb be single and living not very far from her at all.

Even though he'd rejected her, clearly and deliberately, she still could see herself driving to his house, begging him to take her. She'd probably have nightmares about doing that very thing.

She wanted to have more class than that. More pride. Except, God resisted the proud but gave grace to the humble. He gave the humble their wishes while taking from the proud.

God, I've been nothing but humble when it came to Jeb.

Still, it wouldn't be any good now anyway. What if he did accept her? They didn't even know each other. And she didn't have time to do what she'd done before. And he wouldn't.

Walking slowly forward, her dress swishing around her ankles, she went to the pew where the girls had made room for her at the end, and sat down, her back straight, her eyes forward. She would make it through. She always made it through.

Chapter 2

Jeb stood straight and tall beside the casket. It was the least he could do for Donna, who maybe hadn't been so good to him but who had given him the ability to be good to the woman he loved.

Of course, he'd made a much bigger sacrifice than he originally intended when she first asked him to marry her.

Their marriage had lasted a lot longer than it was supposed to, since Donna had lived a lot longer than she originally thought she was going to.

When they first got married, Jeb had wondered if that had been a deliberate deceit, but after seventeen years, he was fairly certain it wasn't so.

It wasn't like he could blame her for what happened.

He jerked his head at another well-wisher.

Donna had gotten her wishes—all of them; he had seen to it, keeping his word.

None of that would have been possible without his sacrifice, though.

Of course, Donna had allowed him to use her money, although he'd only used it for two things.

His farm was paid for because of Donna.

And he'd kept his promise to Clay Stryker.

He wasn't sure he would have married Donna otherwise.

More well-wishers, more head nodding, and the occasional thank you. Jeb stood with his jaw set, his feet planted.

Crowds were not his thing. He hated standing up in front of everyone, hated having their eyes on him. Hated being where everyone could see him.

He'd much rather be wearing his old blue jeans and work boots and be out with his cows.

Driving a tractor in the field somewhere.

But there were occasions in a man's life where he had to do what needed to be done, and he didn't have a choice.

Funerals were one of those things.

At least Donna had given specific instructions for what she wanted, so there was nothing left for him to do other than attend and make sure her wishes were carried out, for the last time.

After the service, the casket would be wheeled out and taken to the graveyard.

She didn't want people following and had specifically requested that there be a meal afterward instead while they laid her in the ground and covered her up.

In the meantime, Jeb would have to eat, have to be in the same room with Lark.

He'd managed to avoid her since that fateful day when she asked him to marry her, and he'd had no choice but to turn her down.

What other answer could a thirty-year-old man give an eighteen-year-old girl?

It was the only answer that made sense. Even though it wasn't the answer he wanted to give. He might have answered differently, even still, but he'd given Clay his word.

Plus, tongues already wagged about her working for him, and if they ended up getting married, they'd want to know what all had been happening while she had been underage on his farm.

He didn't really want those questions, even though he was completely innocent and could answer everything honestly, by the grace of God.

Even now, the hairs on the back of his neck tingled, despite the fact that he couldn't see her, hadn't seen her since he glanced back and saw her walking up the aisle, wearing a dark green dress with black trim, the waist nipped in, emphasizing her slimness, flaring out around her hips, twirling and teasing slim ankles with each step she took.

He was used to seeing her in blue jeans and a T-shirt, except for that white dress. The one that floated through his dreams. The one that had made his heart lodge in his throat and his normally slow tongue tie itself in knots.

He was just as bad now. It was like he hadn't matured at all.

"We're ready to begin the service whenever you are, Mr. Malone." The pastor spoke low and respectfully beside him, making Jeb's head jerk.

He'd been deep in thought, but not about his wife.

He nodded his head, never able to get his tongue to work the way he wanted to, and took a last look at the woman he'd been married to for the last decade and a half.

He hadn't expected to be married more than six months, and yet somehow seventeen years had gone by.

He regretted it, regretted most of it, but it was too late. And he wouldn't want Donna to know how much he wished he had said no when she had made her offer.

So what if he had lost the farm?

Of course, Lark wouldn't be a vet now, and from everything that he'd heard, she was a great one and quite happy without him, so maybe he would do it all again.

With a last look at Donna, he nodded for the ushers to close the casket lid, and without a backward glance, Jeb went over and sat down.

It wasn't the woman in the casket he was thinking of. It was the woman halfway back, in the dark green dress, with the straight back and the long mane of hair trailing down behind her.

Once upon a time, she'd been young, and so had he.

Chapter 3

Twenty years ago...

Lark pushed a strand of hair away from her sweaty face as she stepped into the post office in Sweet Water, North Dakota.

Her brothers were all off on harvest crew, and they'd left her little sister, Charlie, and herself home to take care of their mom and the farm.

The boys would stop in periodically over the summer, but for the most part, it was Lark and Charlie who needed to do the bulk of the work. And of course their mom, who always carried more than her share.

The boys sent money home, but Lark knew that things were tight at the house; anybody with a brain knew that a woman raising eight kids on her own after her husband died was not going to have an overabundance of money trying to scrape things together on a hardscrabble farm in North Dakota.

But their mom had given them the best life she could, and Lark intended to pay that back. She just wasn't sure how.

Right now, she was making a post office run for her mom, mailing several letters and purchasing a book of stamps.

So far, her efforts to find a summer job had been unsuccessful, and the last day of school was yesterday.

So, as she stepped into the post office, she went directly to the bulletin board where people posted their want ads, things for sale, giveaways, and help wanted signs.

There wasn't much happening in Sweet Water. It was a small town, with a lot of hardworking country people and not a whole lot of economic opportunity.

So, when a small ripped-off piece of paper in the bottom left-hand corner with the words "help wanted" written in chicken scratch across the top caught her eye, it really caught it.

She squinted, knowing she wouldn't be any good at bookkeeping or caretaking. Although she'd done both of those jobs. And she didn't really want to babysit, but if that was the only thing she could find to do, she'd take it.

But she wanted something different. Something where she could work with animals. Which was hard to find around Sweet Water, other than jobs on ranches. In order to take those jobs, she would most likely have to leave their own farm and travel to them and stay for the summer.

Sweet Water Ranch wasn't hiring. She'd already asked.

She supposed she would not be picky and would just take whatever she could get, but she'd been praying and trying to have faith that if God truly wanted her to be a veterinarian, He'd come up with something to help her get experience working around animals.

She figured a person could probably be a vet with no animal experience, but surely it would help her out to have spent most of her life with them. Plus, that was where God had given her a deep interest—in animals.

Looking closer at the sheet, she saw that whoever had made the ad was tight with his words:

Help wanted.
Low pay, hard hours.
Come to Malone's Dairy to apply.

Malone's Dairy. She was pretty sure she recognized that name. Although she'd never been out to that farm. It wasn't too far from her house, but it was down a lane that she'd never ventured down since it was private.

Still, her heart gave a little stutter step, and she smiled. The feeling that this was exactly what she should do settled over her.

She didn't always feel like that, but a few times in her life, she'd felt like something was just right, and this was one of those times.

Nodding to herself, she decided that on her way back through, she would stop at Malone's Dairy.

It didn't take long to complete her transactions at the post office, and she hopped on the four-wheeler that she used to go from place to place, which wasn't entirely legal, but which had worked for her so far, and her mom, while typically not encouraging them to do things that weren't completely on the up and up, just told her to take back roads.

She did so out of town, having to turn around twice because she'd taken a couple turns she wasn't quite sure about, since she'd never been to Malone's.

But she didn't mind. The wide-open blue sky, with no clouds as far as she could see, the waving grass, and the feeling of being completely free made her feel like she could drive forever and she didn't care whether she got lost or not.

Finally, she came out on the road, on the opposite side from where Malone's Dairy's driveway pulled out onto the state highway. Looking both ways at the completely deserted highway, she crossed carefully and motored slowly down the drive.

She wouldn't want them to think that she was irresponsible by flying up to their house, as eager and excited as she was. In theory, there would be cows there. At the very least. Probably dogs and cats too. Perhaps goats, and if she were really, really blessed, there would be horses as well.

Horses were her favorite, but they'd never really had enough money to own their own.

The perception was that all ranches used horses in the West, but that wasn't true. Horses were expensive, not just to buy but to own. Not only were there feed costs involved, but footcare, every four to six weeks, plus vet care as well.

Horses were a lot more high maintenance than cows, and a four-wheeler's only requirement was gas most of the time. If something broke down on her machine, one of her brothers could usually fix it.

With a horse, the vet almost always had to be called.

Not that Lark minded. She loved when the vet came, because it felt like that was her calling, and when the vet was there, she could watch carefully to see what he did. Their vet, Dr. Ringwald, was old and about to retire, but he didn't mind at all having Lark look over his shoulder.

She was pretty sure that he would have hired her for the summer, if he didn't already have two assistants working for him.

He told her that if he ever had an opening, he'd keep her in mind, and she was sure he was as good as his word. It was just that those openings hadn't happened yet.

The farm buildings came into sight, and she slowed even more. The house was an old two-story farmhouse, white, with an old roof which looked like it needed to be replaced.

There was an implement shed and a larger pole building where they probably kept their tractors and other pieces of equipment.

There was a silage pit not far away, two of them, one that had been completely used, and the other that was only about a quarter full.

Perfect timing, since it looked like it would last the rest of the summer until they filled it up again this fall.

There was a newer building, which looked like it was probably the dairy, since she could see a smaller block building with big windows and a tank sitting inside, which was almost certainly the milk house.

Probably the stable where they used to milk had been torn down when they built the new parlor. It seemed like that was what everyone was doing, investing a lot of money in it, and then since the price of milk had gone down, they couldn't pay back the money they borrowed to improve.

More than one dairy she knew had gone out of business because of that.

She wondered whether she should stop at the house, where the office most likely was, if there was an office that was manned during office hours, which, looking around at the place, she got the idea that there probably wasn't.

There weren't a bunch of people running around. In fact, she didn't see anyone.

And there weren't any vehicles moving, or anything moving, actually.

In fact, the place was rather dead.

Except for the dog who came slowly over to see her, its muzzle gray, its steps stiff and arthritic.

She saw one cat strut through the yard without even glancing in her direction, heading toward the barn, its belly big, like a litter of kittens was due any day.

Beyond that, she could see cows out beyond the barn, black and white. Holsteins, like every serious dairy owned, but no humans, and no activity.

Except, as she got closer, she saw that the implement shed door was open, and maybe there was movement in there. It was dark, shadowed, and she couldn't quite tell, but she squinted harder, and therefore, when the man stepped into the doorway, wiping his hands on a rag before stopping to put it back in his back pocket, his eyes shaded by the brim of his cowboy hat, his shirt tight across broad shoulders, she wasn't quite surprised.

His boots were worn, scuffed, like he had them as long as she'd been alive, and there was a slight pouch across his middle. There would be no six-pack abs there, but her brothers told her the six-pack abs didn't happen unless a guy spent long hours at the gym. Farmers didn't have that kind of time.

She didn't mind. The dude in front of her had a little extra padding around the middle, different from the lanky teen boys at school. It made him look substantial, like he'd lived life and a strong wind wouldn't blow him away.

She liked it. Liked what that said about him—that he wasn't vain, didn't spend hours flexing in front of the mirror, that who he was was more important than what he looked like.

She might only be fifteen, but she had six brothers and already knew she wanted a man of character, the kind of man who would work long hours and would love and care for and provide for his family.

Funny that at the sight of this man, she would start thinking about all the things she wanted in a husband.

She couldn't see his face very well, but from the stubble on his chin, she had a feeling that he was a good bit older than she was.

And she was only fifteen. She had years of high school, college, and vet school stretching out in front of her. She'd never really spent much time looking at boys, because they would just derail the plan she had for her life. She wasn't interested in getting derailed. Not by a boy.

This guy was not a boy.

She parked the four-wheeler beside the truck that sat where the stones of the driveway ended, shutting it off and swinging a leg over.

She wasn't shy, and she never had a problem going up to people and talking to them. Today was no different.

She brushed her hands down her jeans, put her ball cap on straight, pulling her hair out through the hole in the back as she strode toward the man.

"Howdy, mister. I'm Lark." She grinned, smiling at his surprised look, like he wasn't expecting someone to show up today, let alone a high school girl with a big smile on her face.

His befuddled look made her grin grow bigger.

Didn't he remember that he had asked for help on his farm?

"You lost?" the man finally said, staring at her hand like she was offering him a snake rather than friendship.

She kept it out, figuring he'd eventually come around. She had a couple brothers who were a little bit quiet. Sometimes it took them a while to warm up to people. That man put her in mind of those guys, particularly Preacher, who wasn't shy but was less outgoing than her other brothers.

"No. I saw your sign in the post office, and I came right out. I'm looking for a job for the summer. The last day of school was yesterday, and I don't have anything lined up. I babysit, and there's a couple of bookkeeping jobs in town, but I want to be outside. I want to be a vet when I grow up, and working a bookkeeping job isn't going to help me with that at all."

The man lifted his hat and rubbed a hand over his head before settling it back down and staring at her for a moment. He finally spoke.

"It might."

Just two words, but the man's voice was smooth and went down her backbone real easy. She liked the way it felt. Odd, to think about the way a voice felt.

Her hand was still out, and she lifted her brows, a little challenge, friendly though, because her smile never wavered.

"I told you my name's Lark. You gonna introduce yourself?"

"Jeb." He finally took her hand, pumped it once, short and quick and dropped it like it scalded him.

To cover the odd feeling that gave her – hurt? Embarrassment? Irritation? She wasn't sure, but she talked to keep from thinking about it.

"You know, I'll give you that. If I end up with my own business, owning my own practice, I might need bookkeeping skills, but I figure those can be learned anywhere. In college or what have you. But I can't learn about animals while I'm sitting behind a desk."

"So you're just here to learn."

"Is there another reason to be here?"

"Money."

"Well, I want some of that too. Mom has eight kids... You probably know my mom. Mrs. Stryker?"

He lifted a brow, and she took that to be a yes. He didn't have a whole lot of words, but he had an expressive face. She bet he didn't even realize it. It wasn't hard to read at all. He was intrigued with her but cautious. Probably because he was shy, and the idea of a friendly, *female* guest was giving him the urge to turn around and run.

She almost chuckled at that. Obviously, he hadn't given in to the urge, but he did have his feet planted like he was trying to make sure that didn't change.

"I thought you would. Anyway, it's not easy to raise eight kids, and I figured a job here would be close enough to her that I could help, since I'll still have work to do on our farm too. Although my little sister Charlie will be helping as well."

"I see."

"What did you think when you put the sign up in the post office? You looking for someone to milk cows?"

She knew most of the time men didn't enjoy milking cows. She didn't really understand it, because she thought it would be fun. Usually guys wanted to go drive a tractor or something. Something about driving big equipment that kind of appealed to them somehow.

"Yeah," he said slowly as she grinned again. He wasn't answering her questions. Maybe she should ask them slower, since obviously his brain and mouth were missing a few wires, and their signals were slow.

"So, yes, you're looking for someone to milk?"

He nodded. Just a slow jerk of his chin in assent.

"The sign was still up, so I assume you haven't found anyone?" She looked around. "Not to mention there's no other cars in the driveway, so you must still be looking. I'm here." She allowed her grin to be engaging as she lifted her shoulders in a gesture that said he might as well accept the fact that she was here to help.

"Are you twelve?"

Okay. That was a little offensive. She was skinny, sure, and a little bit short, but from the way she acted, most people thought she was older. Although, some people just judged her on her appearance, and those people usually did think she was younger than what she was.

"I'm fifteen."

"No driver's license."

"There are back roads between my house and yours. It'll take a little bit longer than the highway, but I'm not scared. And I'll be sixteen in less than a year."

He huffed out a laugh, interrupting her.

Okay. That was dumb. But it threw her off a little bit with his question about her age. She hadn't figured it would be a problem.

"Right. I get it. Less than a year. Everybody is going to be a year older in less than a year. Unless today is your birthday." She lifted her brows, like she was asking him.

He gave a small shake of his head, barely perceptible, and his lips flattened, like he didn't want to talk about himself.

It was intriguing, and it made her want to see if she could get him to talk to her. But first, she needed to get him to hire her. And then, she needed to work her butt off to prove to him that he didn't make a mistake in hiring someone who looked like they weren't old enough.

"You don't look like you're capable of moving cows around. There isn't much of you there."

It was two sentences, and the most he'd said, even if it was kind of an insult. So, she'd also have to work her butt off to prove that he hadn't made a mistake and that she was capable of doing the job, even though she was short and skinny.

"We have cows on our farm. They're beef cows, but from what I understand, they're harder." She lifted her chin. "You want to give me a trial? Two weeks?"

She didn't want to do this, but she could make another offer, to sweeten the pot, since even though his eyes were in shadow, his face hadn't moved at all and she didn't think she was any closer to getting hired than she had been when she stepped foot on the property. "If someone else comes along asking for a job in the meantime, and you think they can do a better job, you're under no obligation to keep me. That's for a trial time of two weeks."

"Wow."

She wasn't sure exactly what that word was supposed to mean.

Silence wasn't exactly her thing, but she crossed her arms over her chest, just because she was feeling a little defensive, and tried not to tap her toe while she waited for the man in front of her to...think? She wasn't quite sure whether that was it, or whether he was just trying to talk himself into something. Or maybe out of it. She didn't know.

"So what time do you start milking?" she asked, deciding that she might as well just be bold.

"Four."

"Morning and evening?"

He jerked his head up.

"All right, it's ten o'clock now. I'll be back at three thirty, and you can let me know what you want me to do."

She thought maybe one side of his lips twitched, but she wasn't entirely sure. He was a strange one, quiet, but maybe they'd get along okay, since her mom said that she could talk a leg off a magpie, and possibly some wing feathers as well.

She always said it with a smile, so Lark knew she wasn't insulting her, but sometimes in school it was hard for her to sit still and be quiet without running her mouth about stuff.

The way she saw it, it wasn't natural for people to not talk. God had made folks to be social, to need to have that personal interaction. It wasn't natural for humans to sit still and quiet the way they made kids do in school.

At least that was Lark's way of thinking. Somehow, she'd managed to survive, after a few rough years in kindergarten and first and second grade when it was really hard for her to not jabber.

She got in trouble more than once, and while her teachers hadn't been the most patient, her mom had. Thankfully.

Still, Lark couldn't help but think that her ability to talk was going to come in handy, since working with Mr. Malone seemed like it was going to be a one-sided thing. Her doing all the talking, him doing all the listening. But she figured they could make it work. And actually, they might end up making a pretty good team. That was if he hired her.

"I'll see you at three thirty," she said, allowing a smirky grin to cross her face.

Again, it almost seemed like Mr. Malone's lips twitched in return, although she couldn't be sure.

She lifted a hand and he nodded his head, his hat dipping, then she turned and strode back to the four-wheeler.

She had a job.

Chapter 4

J eb stood in the opening of the implement shed, thumbs hooked in his belt loops, his eyes watching the slender girl who had just informed him that she was going to start working for him as she walked away.

He was twenty-seven years old, and he knew talking wasn't exactly something he was good at. He was shy, which wasn't a manly quality either, and he'd learned to live with both disabilities.

But that girl... She was something else.

He turned and walked back in the shed before she got on her ATV, not wanting her to see him staring at her. After all, she got all upset when he asked her if she was twelve. He didn't see what was wrong with that question, but he didn't want to offend her again by staring at her.

Kids like that always wanted to be thought of as older than what they were, but he'd taken his best guess.

Still, she intrigued him, and he tried to tamp that feeling down.

She was going to be working for him; it looked like that was what she decided she was going to do, anyway, since he never really said he was going to hire her, although he did need the help and no one else was knocking the doors down to get to him. If she was, he was going to have to maintain a professional distance at all times. He couldn't afford to be intrigued or to run around smiling at her.

Even if she was cute.

Veterinarian. She probably had no idea how much work it took to be a veterinarian.

Shaking his head, he listened as the four-wheeler motored away. Then he went back to fixing the tractor. Farming on a shoestring, trying to keep the family farm that his parents had bought forty years ago in operation, in the wild and very rugged and inhospitable North Dakota climate, involved a lot of maintenance at home.

His dad had to become a jack-of-all-trades, and he passed that down to Jeb.

His two sisters had long since left the farm, and he'd bought their shares. They'd been a good bit older than him, in their teens when he had been born, and he wasn't close to them.

He'd been a surprise to his parents, but a handy one it seemed, since he'd been around to help on the farm his entire life.

Both of his parents passed away within a month of each other the year he turned eighteen, almost as though his mom had given up on life when his dad died of a heart attack.

Finding love like that might have been nice, but that would have meant having to talk to people, and he never did. He went to school, did what he had to do, and came home. Some days, he didn't talk at all. Then he graduated and never spoke unless he needed to talk at the feed store.

That wasn't exactly normal, but he was happy with it. Happy with his cows, happy with his farm, and while he missed his parents, he had learned to live alone.

Sure, like normal people he had times of loneliness, but he was content. He just needed help, especially over the summer when he would need to be in the field, he needed to make sure that there was someone reliable around who could milk the cows, by themselves if necessary, so he could get the field work done. Or to help him with the field work, too.

North Dakota summers were notoriously short, and a lot of work needed to be done in a small amount of time.

Still, the girl was young, and maybe she was just pulling a prank. She'd smiled the whole time she was there and seemed almost too good to be true.

By the time three o'clock rolled around, and he'd finished fixing the tractor and had gone out and mowed some hay, he talked himself into the idea that the girl wasn't going to show.

He almost stayed out in the field until four, but something nagged at him, just a feeling, and he pulled into the shed at three twenty-nine according to the clock in the console.

He just had a flip phone, hadn't gotten into the newfangled stuff, one he typically kept in a shirt pocket, if he had a flannel on, which he did most of the year.

June, maybe, July and August, he mostly wore T-shirts.

The rest of the year, at least two layers were necessary, and sometimes a lot more.

So, he could hardly leave a number on the paper, since he didn't sit by the phone all day, and half the time in the summer, he didn't have one with him.

It was just easier to send people out to see him.

So he couldn't call, either, to see if the girl was still coming or to tell her not to bother.

He was torn between which of the two he wanted to do.

He hated making phone calls, so he ended up doing nothing.

And he was half surprised, half aghast when just as the clock hit three thirty, he looked up and saw a cloud of dust along the horizon down the driveway.

As he squinted, the four-wheeler came into view, the girl on it, her hair blowing in the wind, her baseball cap on backward. Still smiling.

She wore the exact same outfit she had on before, jeans and a T-shirt, but as she parked, he could see that she changed her cowboy boots over for muck boots.

Someone had either given her a clue that cows were a little different in the dairy barn than out in the field, or she actually had a head on her shoulders.

He wasn't sure what to say.

So, as usual, he didn't say anything.

"All right. I told you I'd be here. Was that two-week idea okay with you? Because, if it's not, and you just want to hire me right away, that's fine too. I told my mom I told you that, and she said that seemed fair to her. Then, I thought about how I am kinda small, and I don't know anything about dairy cows, so it serves me right if I couldn't learn. And it seems silly for you to have to pay to teach me. Although, that is kind of what corporate people usually do."

"This is a farm."

What he was thinking didn't often come out of his mouth, but he was able to push those words out. It was best that she understood that this was no corporate boardroom, and there were no free handouts. He really couldn't afford to hire someone, but he needed to. A one-man operation wasn't typically very profitable, and his was no exception. But as long as he made enough money to pay the mortgage payment and any feed bills he had, which he tried to keep down, he could make enough to survive. He was very cheap to feed. He could drink a glass of milk and eat buttered toast and a couple of eggs, and be completely happy.

Of course, steak was nice once in a while. Maybe on his birthday.

"I know. That's why I said that if you don't want to pay me, it's fine. Anyway, we can talk about that later. It's time to get started, and I don't want to make you late."

He jerked his head but didn't say anything. The cows could wait. They had before, and he was sure they would again. But they did best if they stuck to a schedule.

"Follow me." He didn't know what else to say. Didn't know what to ask. Maybe he should have a form or something for her to fill out, but he didn't even have that. When he was a kid, anyone who worked on the farm got paid cash. Things had probably changed since then, but he wasn't sure.

For the last two years, he had a friend from high school come out and help him. Before that, he had several locals, and they'd all gotten paid cash.

But being a farmhand wasn't exactly a lucrative life choice, and all the guys had moved on.

His friend stayed in touch, but considering that friendship with him was a long-running, one-sided conversation a lot of times, he didn't talk to them too much.

Not to mention, he worked too much to have time to hang out anywhere.

Farms were like that.

"So, how many cows do you milk? My mom asked me all about it when I got home, and I couldn't answer any of her questions. She's going to want to know tonight, and hopefully I'll come back with a little bit more information."

Lark chattered on, without giving him a chance to answer any of her questions. She went from her mom saying that she would drive her out if it rained, to crossing the bridge whenever it snowed, to saying that when she started school, she wouldn't be able to stay late in the mornings but would have to be home by seven o'clock so she could be ready to get on the bus at seven thirty, at least until she got her driver's license. Then she went off on a tangent about how early that was, and how the school district was borderline child abuse for making her get on the school bus at such an ungodly hour.

He had to bite back a laugh at that. It was such an ungodly hour, and yet she was going to get up at three thirty in the morning to drive out and work for three hours before it was time to get on the bus. Her logic wasn't making sense, but he didn't try to correct her, because that would have involved him having to talk a little faster than what she did, and that was never going to happen.

When she finally stopped to take a breath, he said, "A hundred and twenty."

"What? Hundred twenty what? Gallons?"

Jeb had no idea where she got the idea that he was going to start spouting off the number of gallons of something. What did she think he was talking about a hundred and twenty gallons for? He wasn't sure. Maybe they weren't going to be able to get along, since neither one of them seemed to be able to have a conversation with the other.

"Cows."

"Oh! Cows! That's how many cows you milk."

He nodded, then said, "Got twenty dry right now."

"Dry?" She looked at him with her brows drawn.

This was going to be harder than he thought. He stopped moving, because talking and moving at the same time was harder than just talking.

He looked over the ground, and she started up again, "If you don't want to tell me, that's fine. Mom says I talk too much, ask too many questions, and generally make a nuisance out of myself. I already told you her magpie quote, and she says that pretty much every day. I know she doesn't mean anything by it, so she's not being mean or anything."

Lark continued to chatter. If they were going to get along, she was going to have to give him space. He needed time to think. Time to form his sentences and get the words out. He wanted to. He didn't want to just grunt and point. But she moved too fast, and she left him feeling just a little bit dizzy.

Like he was the child, and she was the adult.

"How old are you?" he finally said, knowing she'd told him before, but needing the reminder for himself.

"Fifteen. But I'm able to—"

He put his hand up again.

He was twelve years older than she was. That was forever.

Chapter 5

J eb swallowed. He could do this. In school, he'd figured out that sometimes he just needed to give his mouth permission to start going, even if it took his brain a little while to engage. Sometimes he ended up coming off with some really weird things, but sometimes he could actually carry on a conversation, without even knowing that his mouth was doing it.

It was like a knee-jerk reaction, only it was his mouth.

Maybe he could start doing something like that again.

Whatever it was, he needed to start using his words.

"Cows that are dry are cows we're not milking. We dry them off to give them a break before their lactation cycle starts again."

Her brows went up, and her chin did too. He thought maybe she didn't know that.

She opened her mouth, but he put his hand up again. He kind of liked the whole hand thing. It worked. He put his hand up, she closed her mouth.

He wasn't sure whether he had been trained, or whether she had.

Regardless, he said, "You don't have to milk in the morning."

"I want to!" She spoke before he could say anything else. "I want to do as much as I can. You don't have to pay me, I just want the experience with the animals. I promise, I'll be invaluable, and you'll even be able to sleep in some—"

He put his hand up again. Her mouth snapped closed. His eyes glinted, and she smiled.

It felt like they shared a joke.

It was an odd sensation, but a crazy feeling of...camaraderie, of finding...someone who got him, ripped through his soul. He hadn't felt that much in his life, hadn't related to people much at all. But Lark, Lark seemed to...give him time, think that he was more than just someone standing and staring, like maybe he had a brain after all, even if he didn't talk much.

It was a good feeling and one he wanted to stow away to examine later, but he had to continue on. Her mouth didn't stay closed long, even with his hand up.

"Fine. You can come."

Her grin got big, and for a second, he almost jerked back, because he was afraid she was going to throw her arms around him.

"Don't touch me." He put a finger out, taking a step back, although managing to do it in a reasonable way and not like he was running from her. He kept his hand up, almost like a barrier between them, his finger pointed out like it was a sword and he was holding her at sword tip.

She put her hands up, and hurt crossed her face for an instant. He wanted to comfort her, to apologize, to tell her that he didn't mean to hurt her, but of course the words didn't come, and she bit her lip.

"I'm sorry. I get excited, and I do have a tendency to hug people, but I'll try to remember that you don't like that. The same way you don't like to talk."

He swallowed. That wasn't true. He couldn't even begin to address the first, but he could say something about the second. "I just need to think first."

Her brows went up, and then she nodded slowly.

"And you're a little bit shy. But that's okay, because I think that you and I will work together really well, since I'm not. Mom says—"

He was shy. But he put his hand up again. "Follow me."

He didn't need her to be rubbing it in, that he had all these problems that normal people didn't.

"This is the milk house. Before we start to milk, we sanitize everything, including the line. This is how you do it."

He showed her the knob on the side of the electrical box, where all the controls were. He pointed to where it said "sanitize," pulled the knob out, lined up the lines, and pushed it back in again. People were going computerized, but when his dad had redone everything and turned his stable into a parlor, the computerized things were just too expensive. This mechanical stuff had worked well, and he couldn't complain. Not to mention, he could work on this, but he wasn't sure whether he'd be able to fix the computerized stuff or not.

He didn't bother to explain all that to Lark. Maybe eventually he would feel more comfortable talking with her, maybe the words would come easier. But in the meantime, he just went around, pointing to the sink, saying that's where they washed the milkers after they were done. She'd understand why after she milked a hundred and twenty cows. Cows weren't exactly potty trained.

He showed her how to turn the tank on so that the milk was stirred. They couldn't put warm milk in with cold milk without stirring it.

They walked out of the milk house, and he took her into the parlor, explained how the cows came in, in short sentences. Ones that he was able to form in his head and get out of his mouth.

Lark listened raptly to every word, looking at him like he'd hung the moon and stars.

He was sure that wasn't what she was thinking. He was just explaining how to milk cows, not expounding on the theory of relativity or anything like that.

Still, her expression made him feel something that he never really felt before. Maybe how it felt to be admired. He wasn't sure. Whatever it was, he thought that if this was the way she made him feel every time she came, he would certainly be looking forward to seeing her come down the driveway.

He explained how they let the cows in, and then he took her over to feed the calves. He had about twenty of them that had been born that year so far, ten that were still on the bottle.

Spring was the big calving time, and although he didn't bother to tell her, they wouldn't usually have that many bottle-fed calves.

He showed her how to mix the bottles up, how to give the bigger calves milk replacer in buckets, and showed her the calves that he was training to drink from a bucket.

Lark seemed to be a natural with the calves. They could be exasperating at times, because cows weren't exactly smart, nor were they easily trained.

He'd gotten impatient more than once trying to teach a six-week-old baby how to drink from a bucket.

He didn't think Lark was going to have that problem.

He was also pretty sure that as long as Lark was working for him, he'd probably just fed the calves for the last time.

He explained how they cleaned the pen and then said that it was time to get the cows.

He went through all of the steps, from bringing them in, to showing how to feed them, to showing how they lined up to go in the parlor.

By that time, the sanitation system was long since finished, and they unhooked the milkers and carried them in, hooking them up to the stations in the parlor.

Most parlors kept the milkers right at the stations, but their parlor was one of the older varieties, and they still carried their milkers from the milk house.

He supposed there were lots of different ways to do it, and more than once, he wished that his dad had had the foresight to set the sanitation stations up right where they milked, so there would be no milkers to carry.

Regardless, it was just one more thing he didn't go into with Lark.

He had to give her credit; it could be a little intimidating. Cows were large, and it hurt when they kicked, but Lark didn't seem scared, and it didn't take her long until she was washing cows and putting milkers on like an old hand.

Certainly by the time they were done, she was holding her own and keeping up with him just fine.

Having someone else in the parlor halved the work, and he'd forgotten how nice it was to have someone working with him. When he needed to run out, either to push more cows in or to untangle one that had gotten twisted around the wrong way, work still continued inside the stable. So, even though they had gotten a late start, they were done right on time.

He showed her how to take the milkers back over, how to wash them, and how to hose down and sanitize the parlor.

He did explain a little bit on how important it was to try to keep germs out, because it could be devastating to have certain diseases run through the herd.

"Are you sure that's it?" Lark asked as he shut the lights off in the milk house and they walked out together.

She was filthy, with manure on her jeans and on her arms, and she even had a spot on her face, which he was not going to tell her about or attempt to clean for her. She could figure it out when she got home.

"Yeah." There wasn't anything to do until tomorrow morning, when they did it all again.

"What are you going to do this evening?" she asked as she matched her stride to his, and they walked toward the four-wheeler.

"I work until dark."

"Doing what?"

"There's a tractor that needs more work, and I need to change the head on the haybine. I need to get the tedder ready for tomorrow morning and make sure the rake and baler are working. First time I've used them this year."

He'd made some haylage already but needed dry hay to feed as well. That's partly why he'd advertised for help. Baling hay was labor-intensive, and he liked to make it into small bales so that he could put it in the mow, and from there, he could throw it down to where the dry cows were. Typically, he fed the dry cows from the loft. That helped them not to twist.

He'd give the big round bales to the whole herd, which wasn't hard to do with the skid loader in the shed.

He didn't explain all of that to Lark, figuring that if she stuck around, she'd figure it out eventually.

"We're making hay tomorrow?"

He hadn't checked the weather all day. Lark had really thrown him for a loop.

But he liked her. Her chatter went down easy on his ears, and she didn't make him feel like he had to answer. She didn't make him feel like he was dumb for not answering, either. Or like he needed to have some kind of smart answer or make her laugh, or know exactly what she was talking about. She just kept on going, and it didn't bother her at all if he didn't feel like joining in.

But she stopped immediately when he raised his hand.

"You need to stop that, pulling one lip up like that, or I'm going to start thinking you're smiling. It'll give me a big head, if I come out here and teach you how to grin." She grinned at him, and there was no flirt in her words. She was just making conversation.

She's only fifteen. There would not be any flirt.

He reminded himself of that, even as he thought that she was probably the person in the world he got along with the best, and he'd only known her for a day.

"Planning on it, if it doesn't rain." He looked up, like he could tell what the weather would be tomorrow just by glancing at the sky.

"All right then, I'll see what's going on our farm, but if Charlie can take care of things, I'll plan on being out here for the day." She lifted a hand in farewell and walked off in the direction of her four-wheeler before he could say anything.

He wanted to tell her that if it was raining, she wouldn't have to worry about driving her four-wheeler or waking her mother up. He could pick her up. But he couldn't get that out. And it seemed to be settled that she was coming back tomorrow, to milk and to bale hay, whether he wanted her to or not.

He wasn't sure how he felt about that.

Actually, he knew exactly how he felt about it. He was happy.

But she was only fifteen. He...was single. Unattached. And she was friendly and sweet, and...he liked her.

He supposed he didn't really need to worry about her falling in love with him, since he wasn't exactly the kind of man that women fell over themselves to get to. He was more worried about himself. Because he felt like Lark had all the power in the world to hurt him worse than anyone ever had.

The thought scared him.

Chapter 6

T he next morning, Lark motored in to the farm at three thirty AM. Her mother had warned her to not be too early, that she might wake Jeb up, since he might be the kind of man who got up at five till four to be at work at four o'clock.

But she didn't want to be late. So, she got up at three o'clock and left her house at three fifteen.

It was still pitch dark, with just a hint of light on the eastern horizon, as she shut the motor off and sat on it for just a moment.

It was chilly, and she had a hooded sweatshirt on with the hood pulled up and the strings tied.

Her fingers were cold, but that was nothing new. She spent the whole winter with her hands and feet cold, so she didn't even think about it.

But she did wonder whether she should go in and try to do everything that Jeb had shown her how to do, or whether she should wait for him.

It was only her second day.

There was a dim light on in the kitchen, but it looked like the light over the sink or something, from the glow on the front porch, and she didn't want to assume he was awake.

She decided that she was going to go see what she could do, when a figure materialized out of the shadows.

"You coming?" he said, his voice coming out of the darkness, and she caught a faint whiff of...something.

He hadn't come from the house, so that led her to believe that he'd been up and doing something.

"Do you have pigs?" she asked. The only time during the day where she had a tendency to not talk quite as much was first thing in the morning.

Her mom and her brothers teased her that it took a little while for her to get her motor running.

That's what happened when a person had brothers. They thought of things in terms of motors and noises. And gas. There was a lot of gas when one grew up with six brothers.

"I didn't show them to you yesterday."

So that was a yes. "You fed them already this morning?"

"Last night after you left, my sow had twelve piglets. I took the runt inside with me."

"Is it still alive?"

She no sooner asked than he pulled his button-down to the side, and a little snout poked out of the neck of his T-shirt.

He tugged the neck down, and she saw the most adorable little piglet.

"Oh my goodness," she breathed, throwing a leg over and jumping off the four-wheeler, moving forward before she thought about it, and putting a finger on the tiny, warm body.

The way he moved quickly away from her, putting his finger up and telling her not to touch him yesterday, popped into her brain, and she stepped back quickly. "I'm sorry. I didn't mean to get so close."

His eyes clouded for a second before understanding dawned.

He looked down, and she regretted her words, because before she had spoken them, she thought he had an almost...adoring look on his face, like seeing her with the piglet was cute or something.

Now his toe scuffed in the ground before he planted his feet and looked up.

"We need to get something straight."

"I know. I'm not supposed to touch you. I get it." She didn't really get it. She'd known people who didn't want to be touched or whatever, and she knew it was a thing. And everyone said that Jeb was a little bit odd. She didn't really consider him strange, just God made him a little different, and she enjoyed his quirks. After all, if someone could put up with all of her talking, all of her insane cheerfulness, even at three thirty in the morning, then she could put up with a few quirks of her own, couldn't she?

"I'm a man."

She wasn't going to argue with that. She kept her mouth closed, figuring out yesterday that sometimes it took him a little while to say what he needed to say, especially when it was a little bit personal. Talking about equipment and cows and milking and farming seemed to be a lot easier for him than talking about personal things, even something simple like what time she should show up for work.

"You're a girl."

She waited.

"We're here by ourselves."

All right. She understood what he was saying. And she supposed it was actually necessary. She couldn't deny that she found Jeb handsome. She found him intriguing as well, and while she was only fifteen, she had brothers. She knew how men thought, at least she thought she did.

"I don't want there to be anything whispered about us. Or said about us, or anything to be true about us."

It was an awkward conversation and an awkward way for him to say it, but she understood that he had a lot riding on the line.

"You'll get in big trouble. I get it. I know someone who's in jail because some girl accused him of something. Sorry. I never even thought."

It was true she hadn't, even if she had admired him and thought about how intrigued she was by him.

"I won't do anything inappropriate. I promise." The promise came easily to her lips, and she remembered what her brother Clay, also known as Preacher, always said. "Don't make promises you can't keep."

She wanted to be known as someone who kept their word, and she wanted to keep that promise, but as soon as she said it, she wished she would have said that she would try. After all, she didn't want to make a promise that turned her into a liar.

He jerked his head. "It just needed to be said," he mumbled.

She nodded, then she pointed at the pig. "Is she gonna make it?"

"I think so. I just need to keep her warm."

"Have you been feeding her?"

This time, there was no doubt that one side of his mouth turned up as he turned tender eyes toward her. How was she supposed to remember that she was supposed to stay away from him when he looked at her like that?

"You want my pig, don't you?"

They weren't exactly romantic words, although he said them in such a way that she had to stifle a giggle.

"Maybe." She lifted a shoulder. She wouldn't mind raising a pig. Wouldn't mind trying her hand at that. Plus, she was adorable.

"Pigs take a lot of work. You have to feed them every two hours, and they need to be kept warm."

"Will she make it if she goes back with her mom?"

"I don't know. The other ones are going to get stronger and stronger, and she probably won't keep up with them. Although, back when my mom was alive, she turned the runts into some of the best pigs we'd ever had."

"I suppose once you get them started, all you have to do is feed them, and they'll eat as much as they can and grow fast."

"That's probably it. Mom had a way with animals too."

She lifted her eyes, meeting his, and she felt like he had just given her a compliment. The way he said it, like he admired his mom and had compared her to her, made Lark's heart beat just a little bit faster.

"Do you want to try?"

"I'd like to."

"I'll give her to you after we're done milking, okay? That way, you don't have to carry her around the whole time. I didn't take the time to dig up the heating pad this morning. I just grabbed her out of the pen and kept her with me."

"All right. I think we have a heating pad at home. Can I take her home?"

"You think your mom's gonna be okay with you having a pig in the house?"

"I've taken lots of things in the house. Including birds, they seem to be my favorite animal. Although, that's really all we had for a while aside from our beef cows, and they're not a smart thing to fall in love with, because then you end up eating them, and your brothers end up teasing you whenever you sit at the table and cry while they pass your pet around on a plate. So, I needed to fall in love with other things. Something we weren't going to eat."

"You chose birds."

"Yeah. I did. I doctored a lot of them. Some of them stuck around, and I still see them."

"I see. Didn't you ever lose any?"

"Yeah. I've lost more than I've saved. But I can't not try, you know?"

He nodded, and she felt like he really did understand. Maybe he did. Maybe he knew what it was like to try to save an animal when you knew that the animal probably wasn't going to make it, but you just couldn't not try.

Whether he got it or not, she felt like he did, and that made all the difference.

They turned together and walked toward the barn. It might be an interesting day, trying to work and carry a pig around the whole time, but maybe she could run home and grab a heating pad.

She put those thoughts out of her head, trying to concentrate on doing her very best and not messing anything up. She didn't want to give him any reason to fire her, because she thought this could quite possibly be the best job she'd ever had in her entire life.

Chapter 7

Lark patted the head of Wilma, her pig. She'd wanted to call it Wilbur, after the pig in *Charlotte's Web*, but it had been a girl. So she settled on Wilma.

Summer had flown past, and tomorrow she started school.

Normally she enjoyed school, enjoyed hanging out with kids and chatting, seeing her friends, and participating in all the fun activities, but this year, she had dreaded it.

The short summer had flown by too fast, and she'd had such a great time. She worked with animals more than she worked with them in her entire life, and she loved it. She got to see the vet do several surgeries: a twisted stomach and a C-section.

She even got to help.

It had been...a magical summer.

"You put a hummingbird feeder up!" she said as Jeb walked out beside her. He still didn't talk much, although he seemed to have gotten a lot more comfortable with her and talked more now than he had at first. He also smiled more, too. She'd actually taken it upon herself to try to do something every day that would make him smile. Whether it was a joke, or whether she brought their lunch, or whether she brought his favorite drink out for him. He claimed for a long time it was water, and then he said he liked iced tea, and then she realized that every once in a while, he treated himself to a Mountain Dew.

So, every once in a while, she brought him a Mountain Dew and a chocolate milk for herself which was her favorite drink.

Sometimes they sat on the cement flower planters outside the milk house and drank their drinks after the work was done. Often on Saturday nights.

The flower planters were bare, because no one had planted anything in them since his mother died. Next year, she planned on doing it herself.

She hadn't told Jeb, but she knew he wouldn't care.

Lots of little things like that he left to her. Just happy to see the things she did. Actually, she got the feeling that a lot of times he liked having someone else around, someone doing little things that he didn't have time for or didn't think about.

They worked together just as well as she thought they would. She'd never worked with anyone who was so sweetly considerate, who did little things to make her life easier, never saying anything, just doing them, never expecting her to do anything in return, although anytime she noticed, it always made her want to do more for him.

She brought his Mountain Dew and her chocolate milk, and they sat on the flower planters.

Tomorrow she'd go back to school. No more hot summer days making hay, or chopping haylage, or fixing tractors, or planting alfalfa.

None of that would have happened if Jeb had gone with his gut and turned her away the first day she came. She had to admit, he would have been better off hiring a boy. She wasn't as strong, wasn't as tough, and Jeb had ended up doing a lot of things to make her work easier. If he'd have hired a boy her age, Jeb was the one who would have had things made easier for him.

"Thanks a lot for taking a chance on me," she said, not really expecting an answer.

He grunted and then took a swig of his Mountain Dew.

They sat there in companionable silence for a while. Gratitude made him uncomfortable and made him even more tongue-tied than he usually was.

"When did you put that hummingbird feeder up?" she asked, knowing if she waited long enough, he would answer that question. It was the ones where he had to think about how he felt that really tripped him up.

"Earlier today while you were feeding calves." He shrugged, like it wasn't a big deal. But they had a whole conversation last week talking again about how much she loved birds and how she had a hummingbird feeder at her house and had been making sure that it was filled up because hummingbirds needed a lot of energy at the end of summer so that they could make the long tens of thousands of miles trip to their South American wintering spot.

"Did you go into town and get it?"

"Ordered it online."

That was a major thing, since his internet wasn't very good, and he had an old dinosaur of a computer that they'd gotten the same time they put their parlor in to keep spreadsheets on.

The Internet was slow, and half the time, the computer didn't work. The fact that he'd taken the time to sit down and order it meant a lot.

His phone was a flip phone, and the only thing it did was call and send texts if one was willing to be patient enough to hit the button four times to get the right letter.

"Well. Have you seen any hummingbirds?" she asked, wondering if they would even show up on a farm. She had no idea.

"Not yet. They'll come."

He sounded confident, and she figured he was probably right. Somehow they'd sense the nectar, and they'd show up. Maybe not a whole lot this year, but if he kept at it, he'd see a good many.

"Where do you have the stuff? I'll make sure I fill it up whenever it's empty."

"I didn't get it to make more work for you." He paused, and then, in an uncharacteristically wordy moment, he said, "You already do more than I pay you for."

The pay wasn't that good. When she thought about all the hours that she worked, and all the money she made, it wasn't worth it at all, except it was to her. She loved the experience she got with the animals, and she couldn't imagine working with anyone who was better than Jeb. She couldn't exactly say that, because she'd never forgotten the conversation that they had about him being a man and her being a girl.

Although, she'd turned sixteen not that long ago. She'd invited him to come to her house for cake and ice cream, which was all the party they had, just family. That was enough.

He declined, as she thought he would.

She hardly ever saw him in town. Once in a while, he came to church, but that wasn't even something he did often either. Although, once one evening in July, when she had to come back because she'd left the bag of milk replacer that she used to feed Wilma, she knocked on the door, and when he answered, his Bible had been sitting on the table, like he'd been just sitting there reading. There'd been a notebook beside it, but she wasn't quite brave enough to walk across the kitchen floor to see what he had been writing.

She got the milk replacer and left, but the sight of his Bible on the table, the small light burning, and the idea that in the evenings that's what Jeb did, sat at the table and read his Bible, had been burned into her mind.

She'd never heard him use bad language, and he certainly didn't tell off-color jokes. And true to his word, he never touched her. Not even to help her up and down on a wagon or in and out of a tractor.

She could admire someone who lived what he believed, and that was definitely a way to describe Jeb.

"What will you do with yourself all day long when I'm not here?"

"Enjoy the silence," he said, but he didn't sound like he was looking forward to it, and she figured that was just his way of not being dramatic about her leaving.

"I have something for you."

She jerked her head over, looking at him. She wouldn't have thought he was sentimental, but it almost seemed like he was giving her a gift because she was starting school?

"I missed your birthday," he said, holding up a cardboard box and handing it to her. "Sorry it's not wrapped."

She laughed, hardly able to imagine Jeb trying to figure out how to wrap a present.

"It doesn't matter," she said, surprised she hadn't noticed the box before. It had been sitting behind him in the flower planter, and she wondered if he planned all of this, although he couldn't have known that she was bringing soda. Except... He seemed to know her, without saying anything. Knew when to gently tease her and when to be quiet. He probably knew her well enough to know that she would consider this a special day, one where she would bring them each a drink and they would sit and do their little quiet celebration.

"You didn't have to do anything." She knew money was tight and felt a little bad that he'd spent even a little bit on her.

"I wanted to." He didn't say anything else, but his words sent a shiver down her spine and made her stomach do a slow churn.

No. He didn't mean it the way it sounded. He was just being a friend.

Maybe it was a good thing she was going back to school, because she had to remind herself of that more often as the summer went by.

He seemed like he trusted her more and didn't try to move away when she got too close.

It was like he believed her when she said that he would never have to worry about that with her.

She hadn't forgotten that promise.

She swallowed. "My goodness. I can't begin to imagine what it might be."

"Don't get your hopes up. It's nothing special."

She tilted her head and looked over at him, grinning. "Any gift is special. Just the idea that someone thought about me long enough to get me something. It means a lot."

In her family, no one got big gifts, it was just the idea that people remembered. Maybe they picked up something that they thought someone would like. Or to give them something that would make their day a little bit more special. Like chocolate chip cookie dough ice cream or a hot fudge sundae. Or a warm, fuzzy pair of socks. A special drink. Something little, but a gift that made life easier, that made someone smile, was a great gift indeed.

But as she peeled back the top of the box, she realized that it wasn't a gift to make her life easier. It was one to make it more beautiful.

Chapter 8

"Did you make this yourself?" Lark asked in an awed whisper as she pulled a professional-looking birdhouse out and held it up, allowing the cardboard box to drop to the ground, while she looked at the exquisite craftsmanship of the birdhouse she held.

"Yeah. It's not that big a deal."

"It is to me. I couldn't begin to buy something like this; it's gorgeous." She held it up, examining it. It looked like he had made three different stories in one birdhouse, with three different entrances, one on each of three sides.

"This side is the one you would put against the fence or the tree wherever you attach it to." He said that as he pointed to the flat side that had no little peg for the birds to stand on.

"I see. That's super neat. So it could have three different bird families in it at one time, and they'd all have their own little private entrance." It was so cute, she couldn't keep from smiling. "Thank you so much. It's...really sweet how you knew how much I love birds, and you thought and took the time to make me something so beautiful that I love."

He nodded. He didn't say anything.

"How long did it take you to make this?"

"I worked on it in the evenings after you left."

He didn't say how long, and she figured maybe he didn't want to admit how long it had taken him.

That was the kind of thing that he seemed to find difficult to talk about. Anything personal like that. Or maybe he just didn't want to.

Of course, maybe that crossed his line of what was appropriate between them.

She supposed she should see him as an older man, but she really didn't. She saw him as a friend. As a good friend. Of course, he was definitely an attractive friend.

"I wish I didn't have to go to school tomorrow. I wish I could just stay here and do this for the rest of my life."

He huffed out a breath. "Your life will be so much more than that. What happened to being a vet?"

"This is better than being a vet. You know what you're going to do every day, and you go out, and you have a purpose. It's... I love it. Love working with the cattle, love working with the calves, the pigs, making hay and turning my face to the sun and wind, then sitting here after a hard day, just chilling and chatting and satisfied that the work is done and it was a good day. I love it all."

"I think it will get old." He said that casually, not like there was something wrong with her for loving it and not like she was naïve and didn't know it. That was the thing about Jeb. He might have seen her as a little girl, but he never treated her like one.

"I don't think so. I can't imagine it getting old. I haven't even scratched the surface of doing what I want to here. Spending as much time as I want."

He didn't say anything for a little bit, but then he added, "There will still be holidays. And next summer."

"You mean you're not going to hire someone to replace me?"

"No one could replace you."

She dropped her jaw and looked at him. But he was looking away and pretended that he didn't see her. Or maybe he just avoided her eyes on purpose. Maybe he didn't want to have to explain himself.

She was definitely reading way more into that than what she should, so she closed her eyes for a few seconds, then looked back at her birdhouse.

"Can I set it up here? Attach it to the far barnyard fence so that we can stand in the parlor and look out the window and see the birds?"

"We'll have to keep that window clean so we can see out of it."

"Clean, and keep it from steaming up. It's done that a few times this summer, and it probably does a lot in the winter."

He nodded like she was right. "Maybe we can keep a roll of paper towels there. Although, when it snows, sometimes the snow comes up and half covers the window."

"Then we'll shovel it out. Although, the birds won't be using the birdhouse in the winter."

"That's true, but I was thinking about putting a feeder not too far from it. So we should be able to see them all winter long out that window."

"Wow. It's going to be a bird sanctuary here," she said, only half joking, because with the birdfeeder and a birdhouse, and who knew what all else, the birds really would love sticking around.

"And it's all your fault."

Then he did his little half grin thing.

Every once in a while, he would smile big for her, but most of the time, it was just that grin that pulled his dimple in and made his eyes twinkle, if she could see them under the brim of his hat. He didn't wear it while they were milking, but as they walked out of the milk house every day, he stuck it on his head.

She did the same with her ball cap. It got in the way in the parlor, if she needed to lean her head close to a cow, so she usually braided her hair and just wore it on the way home to keep her hair from blowing and getting all tangled.

Of course, now she had a driver's license, she just needed to save up money to buy a car.

"Are you sure you don't want to quit?"

He said the words like he'd been thinking about that for a while and maybe that was the whole reason he wanted to sit down and talk to her.

Like he was scared that that was what she was going to do.

"No! I told you, I could do this forever."

"You're not coming in the morning anymore though, are you?"

"Of course I am. Why wouldn't I?"

"That's a lot of work for a kid to do while still in school. Milk cows in the morning, go to school, come home and milk again. Are you sure that's not too much?"

"I'm sure. If it is, I'll tell you, but don't worry about it. I... I typically play volleyball, but I wasn't planning to this year. I'd rather be here."

"I don't want you to miss anything at school because you're here. You have to do everything you usually do."

"Even if I don't want to? You think playing volleyball will serve me well for the rest of my life? I could get an injury that would keep me from being able to work pain-free. You probably are saving me a lot of aches and pains in my adulthood."

"I doubt it."

"Seriously. I didn't like it that much, and I wasn't going out this year, and it has nothing to do with milking cows, other than... I'd just rather milk cows than do pretty much anything at school."

"I don't want you to lose your friends and lose your childhood because you're at the farm all the time."

"This is the best childhood a person could have, except... I'm not a child."

She knew he didn't want to admit that she was getting older, that...she was whatever it was that he was scared of, but there was a part of her that wanted him to know. Maybe not exactly that she was available, but that she was turning into a woman. That wanted him to admire her the way a man admired a woman. There, she admitted it to herself, even if she couldn't admit it to him.

"I know." He sounded resigned, like it wasn't something he wanted to think about, which she already knew.

"That doesn't have to scare you," she said, and for once, she wasn't smiling.

"It kinda does."

"It kinda does scare you or kinda does have to?" There was a big difference in her mind.

"Both."

"I don't understand that. I'm sixteen. There's nothing wrong with me being sixteen, and there's nothing wrong with you looking at me and knowing it."

"Never said there was." He lifted his head, looked her in the eyes, the brim of his hat going up far enough that the sun shone on his face, and she could see his sincerity.

She could also see those gorgeous blue eyes. She saw them in the parlor every day, but they looked different in the sunshine, a little bit lighter, like a blueberry with a little bit of morning dew on them.

There was so much expression in them as well. They said what his words never did.

"When I was fifteen, I understood, but not now. And you know I had a birthday." She indicated the birdhouse she still held in her hands. It was gorgeous, and she didn't want to accidentally hurt it in her anger, but she was angry, she could feel it clear down to her fingertips.

She wasn't even sure why.

"I guess I don't see why there's any difference between fifteen and sixteen."

For the first time since she'd known him, Jeb's slow words, his deliberate way of speaking, bothered her. It made her feel like he'd thought about it and come to the conclusion, hard and fast, that there was no changing it.

But while she wanted to stand up and explain to him that sixteen meant that whatever they did was their business now, that she was almost completely grown up, she also knew that if she did that, he would know that there were thoughts in her head that probably shouldn't be there. Not for a man who was twelve years older than she was.

Her mom would be upset if she knew.

Although, her mom had a way of knowing things that Lark never told her, so it wouldn't entirely surprise Lark if her mom did know.

But she never said anything and she trusted Lark, which Lark appreciated and did not want to lose.

So, while she disagreed with Jeb, to tell him that she disagreed could ruin the friendship that lay between them. It was a solid friendship. Strong. One that felt like it could last a lifetime. At least to her. Of course, what did a brand spanking new sixteen-year-old know about lifetimes?

Probably not much.

"I guess you're right," she finally said, although she heard the note in her voice that said she didn't like it much.

He stood, even though she knew he wasn't done with his soda.

He turned, leaning a hip against the cement planter, and crossed his arms over his chest. His position put him less than a foot away from her, and his nearness made her nervous.

Or maybe it was the look in his eyes.

"You have high school to finish. You have college to go to. You have years of vet school. Don't screw it up."

But she wasn't going to let him tell her what to do. To make her decisions for her. To act like that was the only way.

She hopped off the planter, birdhouse held carefully in one hand, chocolate milk sitting on the flat top, at the corner. She turned toward him, setting the birdhouse down deliberately.

If he was going to turn away, he stopped when he saw her move.

He looked at the birdhouse as she set it down, like he couldn't quite understand what in the world she was doing.

"Maybe that's not what I was meant to do." She crossed her arms over her chest and planted her feet, imitating the pose that seemed to be his favorite. Although he still had his hip resting casually against the planter.

"That's what you wanted to do when you came here."

It was a statement she couldn't disagree with.

"I'm young. I'm allowed to change my mind."

"That's my point."

"Then you're arguing against yourself, because maybe I wanted to be that, but I don't anymore." She still did. Really. But she wanted to be on the farm too. Why couldn't she have both?

"Do you?" He lifted his brows, and that was the thing about Jeb. He didn't move fast, so he waited for her answer. And he'd wait as long as it took.

She couldn't lie. As much as she wanted to, as much as she tried to make the words come out of her mouth, all it did was stretch her neck, because her lips refused to open.

"Yes." She pressed her lips back together, looked away.

"All right then."

She wasn't sure what he was saying all right about. He hadn't said how he felt. What he wanted.

Ask.

He wasn't going to answer. She knew it.

"What do you want out of life?" She still had her arms crossed and looked at him almost defiantly. Her eyes narrowed. "Or aren't you going to tell me?"

Chapter 9

Jeb stared at Lark, her normally happy and carefree face filled with thunderclouds. He hated that they were there because of him.

She didn't seem to understand all the hints that he'd been trying to drop about how he needed to stay away and keep his distance from her. That he was going to fall in love with her, that she was going to break his heart because she was going to leave. She was only sixteen. Too, too young. Way too young.

Too young to have the cares and worries of a farm. Too young to tie herself down there. Too young to be tied up with someone like him, even if she could return his feelings, which he highly doubted. Someone like Lark, happy and carefree, always chattering and brimming with ideas and fun, wanting something as frivolous as a birdhouse, and it made her happy. It had absolutely nothing to do with anything, didn't help the farm any, didn't help feed calves, didn't help pay the bills, it just made her happy.

So very happy.

It had made him happy to see her smile. To see the pleasure settle on her face as she opened it and realized that he spent hours crafting it just for her.

Somehow that had turned into him telling her that she needed to forget about the farm. To live her life. To be happy. To do the things she wanted to do, because if she didn't, she'd regret it.

Of course, he didn't regret any of the things he didn't do. He had wanted to be on the farm, and he never wanted anything else, but it was understandable because of his personality. He was the kind of man who was rock solid, steady. Didn't run around with the wild crowd, never had. Had no interest in them. He just loved going to bed early, getting up, and putting his hand to the plow again.

Lark was different.

And as happy-go-lucky and cheerful as she was, he felt like she was also a lot more fragile than anyone knew. A life of drudgery would wear her down quicker than anything, and she'd hate the fact that he'd allowed her to spend all of her teen years holed up on the farm. Rather than hanging out with her friends, doing all the school activities she wanted to, and having those great memories for herself.

Even though he wanted her here. With him.

He couldn't tell her in plain words, couldn't figure out how to say that he wanted her but couldn't have her.

How to answer her question about what he wanted out of life. This farm.

And Lark.

He took a deep breath and sighed softly. "I'm happy here."

"Then why is it so hard for you to imagine that I would be happy here too?"

He wished. He wished she would be. "Have you ever noticed that you and I are different?"

He almost meant that question seriously, but it was so far out of his realm of thought that she could actually believe that they were the same, could be happy with the same things, that he couldn't keep the incredulity out of it.

"Of course we're different. What does that have to do with anything?"

"So it makes sense that I'd be happy here. You wouldn't be."

"Did you ever notice that we make a really great team?" she asked, still sounding angry.

He blinked and looked away, over her shoulder, at the waving grasses and the deep blue sky and the line of contrast where they met.

He supposed she was right. They did make a good team. A great team. Her with her unflagging optimism, and him with his steadier nature, her with her people skills and outgoing personality, and him, content to be in the background and offer support.

They certainly worked well together on the farm. All summer they'd been together, side by side, and he certainly had enjoyed working with her, although he couldn't believe she felt the same way about him.

"You might be right about that."

"Might be?"

He shrugged.

"We balance each other. We're perfect. I'm outgoing, and you're calm. I like talking, you don't. I run around and see the things that we can do, and you are the steady person behind me that balances me."

"I'm old, and you're young." At that, her lips pressed together, and she looked away. His eyes narrowed at her. "You don't have to lie to try to save my feelings. I don't wish I were younger."

Not really. The only reason that he might wish he was younger was so that he would be more compatible with her. But other than that, he didn't regret his age. Every year, he learned something, every day hopefully. He didn't want to live his life without learning things. Without growing. And that meant that he had years put under his belt.

What he lost in physical abilities, he gained in mental ones. In wisdom. And patience.

"Maybe I wish I was older."

"Don't wish your life away. It'll be gone soon enough."

"You don't have to talk like you're eighty. You're only twenty-seven."

"How do you know how old I am?"

Her cheeks reddened, and he wondered about that. Had she asked someone?

"I was curious." She lifted her shoulder and shrugged, like it didn't matter. "Whatever. Fine. I'm still planning on going to college. And I'll still be a vet. No big deal. I can still work here."

For a while anyway. She couldn't work on the farm forever. There wasn't a vet school close enough for her to commute. If she was going to become a vet, she was going to need to live somewhere other than Sweet Water.

But she could possibly commute to college, if she went somewhere close.

"You're not that old."

He pushed off the planter. He wasn't going to argue with her. He wasn't that old. She was right.

But he was too old for her.

"All right. See you tomorrow morning."

He smiled to himself. She understood without words.

"But if you have someone with milk fever, or if you have a twist, I'm not going to be able to help you, 'cause I have to leave for school." She sighed, picking up her chocolate milk and her birdhouse. "Can I leave this here?"

"You don't want it at your house?"

"No. I can't wait to look out the parlor window and see birds making a nest in it. That'll be a real treat."

"All right. I'll have it up tomorrow morning when you get here."

"I believe you will." She sighed again, and he realized that he'd never given her credit for being older than her age. She was only sixteen, but she didn't act like a sixteen-year-old. She acted like a farm girl, one who'd been raised knowing that life wasn't a bowl of cherries and that a person had to work their way through. That she'd been taught what was right from a young age, and she wasn't frivolous or silly like teenage girls were supposed to be.

Maybe he was being too hard on her, but he knew he wasn't. Not really. She'd be wasting her time with him.

"See you in the morning," she finally said, and he nodded.

"Good night."

Chapter 10

"Thanks so much, Mrs. Smith. I'll see you later," Lark said as she pulled her coat tight around her and walked out into the late April chill.

She hadn't joined the volleyball team, and when her homeroom teacher had tried to get her to run for student council, she'd declined that as well. But when she'd seen that a nursing home team was being assembled, and that they would be making visits during lunch, eating lunch with the residents at the nursing home instead of in the cafeteria, Lark had jumped on the chance.

It was an extracurricular activity which would look good on her transcripts, but it wouldn't take her away from her duties at the farm.

Jeb had been correct. Getting up at three thirty every morning to be out to milk by four had her exhausted most of the time. Especially since immediately after school, she drove directly to the farm, changing her clothes at the milk house.

When she had talked to Jeb about it, he had said it was okay, and then he pretty much avoided the milk house from three thirty to four o'clock, just on the off chance that he might meet her in there with one of her socks off or something.

The man was a prude.

It was irritating, but also endearing, and intriguing as well.

She could see how the guys at school were players. She heard them talking about notching the bedposts and about liking girls who got drunk.

There were a whole bunch of other things they talked about, things she basically tried to ignore, but it just made Jeb all the more appealing. He wasn't like those other boys. He was completely different. And she could see easily that once he gave his loyalty, he would be loyal forever. He wouldn't want to notch bedposts, he would want to make a home. That was what she wanted too.

Stepping out into the cold, she walked to the small car she'd been able to purchase over Christmas. Her brothers had helped her pick it out and had chosen one that they thought would run well for her. So far, they'd been right. Although it was going to need tires before next winter.

But that was several months away, and she'd cross that bridge when she came to it.

She parked her car in the school parking lot and jumped out, looking at her watch. She had about seven minutes until the bell rang for class.

There were five members of the nursing home club, so each of them had an assigned day of the week to eat lunch with the residents.

She'd happily do it more often too.

She loved her older friends and had a lot in common with them, maybe because she had so many older siblings, but she really felt like she could relate to adults better. The things her classmates talked about didn't seem that important to her, and sometimes she had to bite down hard on her tongue when they got all upset about stuff that in the long run really didn't matter.

It made her feel like she didn't belong, that there was something wrong with her because she just wasn't the same as everyone else.

She never felt that way when she was out on the farm with Jeb. Milking cows, baling hay, fixing something, it didn't matter how cold it got, how much the wind blew, how much snow they got, it always felt like home when she stepped onto the farm.

If only she could get Jeb to notice her, but unfortunately, she wasn't any better at that than she was at relating to kids who were her age.

"Hey! Lark! Wait up!"

She stopped short, recognizing her name immediately, since she was the only one in school with that name. She turned to see Brad Chambers jogging over to her.

Brad had had a stellar season on the football team and was heading to college to play, although Lark wasn't sure which college or team. He was a nice, small-town boy with dreams and plans that went beyond Sweet Water, although Lark didn't know much about him at all and was honestly surprised he knew her name. It occurred to her at that point to wonder what he was doing out in the parking lot. He should be at lunch.

"Hey, Brad," Lark said, smiling, because that's just what she did. But she glanced at her watch because she definitely didn't want to be late for class. She loved going to the nursing home and didn't want to lose her position on the nursing home team.

"Hey. You know prom is coming up next month, and... I was, you know, hoping you'd go with me."

Lark blinked.

She knew Brad, knew his name, knew he went to her school. But that just seemed like such a random question. They'd never even talked. He wanted her to go to a dance with him?

Was this how that was done? Two people who had never spoken before went to a dance together?

Maybe she just had things all messed up in her mind, but she just had the idea that people were friends before they were more. Maybe that's not the way it worked with the rest of the world. Sometimes she walked around with her head in the clouds and didn't really pay attention to what everyone else was doing.

"I'm sorry?" she said, just making sure that she heard right. "You want me to go to prom with you?"

"Yeah," he said, smiling like he'd just done her a big favor. But then he said, "I know we don't really know each other. Except I sit behind you in Spanish, and... I guess I'd kinda like to get to know you a little."

Her eyes got big. He was in her Spanish class? She'd never noticed.

She did, however, know how to say Jeb's name in Spanish, if that meant anything. She could also say cow, Malone's Dairy, and "the tractor is broken down" in Spanish as well. Stuff that mattered to her.

Not that she was ever going to talk to or about Jeb or his farm in Spanish, but those were the kinds of things that interested her in Spanish class.

"Um, I guess I hadn't really thought about prom. That's...a dance, right?" She was pretty sure it was, but it was still kind of blowing her away that Brad Chambers, high school football star and person she'd never talked to, wanted to go to a dance with her.

He laughed like she made a joke. "What? Do you want me to get down on one knee?" He said, and he bumped her arm with his and then, to her horror, dropped down on one knee.

"Lark Stryker, would you do me the honor—"

"Get up!" Lark hissed in a whisper that wasn't soft at all as she glanced around the parking lot, hoping no one saw this. They'd think he was proposing to her or something, and the last, very last thing she wanted was for anyone to think that there was something between Brad and her. She didn't want Jeb to hear that.

Although... What did it matter? Jeb didn't care. Jeb wouldn't find out anyway. Jeb didn't run in high school circles. Jeb barely even came into town.

But she wasn't interested in this boy in front of her. She wanted...Jeb. Someone serious. Someone compassionate, someone who noticed that she liked birds and spent hours making her a birdhouse with his own two hands. Someone who saw that she liked taking care of animals and gave her the runt of the litter. Someone who encouraged her to be with her friends but didn't forbid her to do what she knew she was born to do. Wasn't that crazy? Someone who didn't laugh at her for thinking that she was born to milk cows.

"Lark? Are you paying attention?" Brad said, and he sounded annoyed, like he'd asked her once before already.

Jeb had infinite patience. She'd never seen him angry, even when the cows absolutely refused to do what they were supposed to do, or they kicked their milker off ten times in five minutes. He just patiently put it back on. Tried to figure out what the problem was and fix it. He didn't get upset, and he never yelled.

"Lark!" Brad looked at his watch. "I'm going to be late for class." She started walking, and he fell into step beside her. "If you need time to think, that's fine, just say so. But... I mean, come on, is it really that hard of a decision? Were you going with someone else?"

"No. I'm sorry. No... I wasn't going with anyone else. I...wasn't going to go at all. I'm sorry, Brad."

"You said no?" Brad said, and he didn't exactly sound conceited, but he definitely sounded surprised that she would turn him down. She wasn't sure what made him think that she would say yes in the first place. Had she ever acted like she liked him? Had she ever even noticed he was alive? If he hadn't been paraded in front of the entire school as the best football player in Sweet Water, North Dakota, she wouldn't even know his name.

"I did. Not because I hate you or anything, just because...I don't want to go to a dance."

See? She was weird. Everyone wanted to go to dances. But she just didn't see the point. Really, she loved chatting with her friends, but she didn't really like loud music, and didn't want to get all dressed up, didn't want to have to leave the farm early so she could fix her hair or whatever. It just didn't appeal.

"You don't want to go to the *prom*? Wait, you're choosing not to go, and it's not because you don't have a date, because I just asked you."

"Yeah. I'm sorry. I know that's kind of weird, but I just don't want to," she said, shrugging her shoulders and checking her watch. "We're going to be late. We better walk faster."

"Yeah. I guess so. Oh," he said as he speeded up beside her. "So... It's not me? You just don't like dances?"

"That's right. I don't have anything against you. I just have better things to do."

"Better things than a dance?"

"Yeah," she said casually, not wanting to explain that her "better things" was milking cows. Or hanging out at the farm. He wouldn't understand. Most people wouldn't. Even in North Dakota, normal people didn't choose hanging out on the farm over going to a dance.

"So...you want to do something else with me?"

Oh, man. She hadn't even considered he'd ask her that.

How could she tell him that he was just a boy and she wasn't interested in boys who didn't stand tall and silent, work hard every day, have patience that lasted forever, and...weren't Jeb?

"I..." She didn't want to hurt his feelings, but she didn't want to do anything with him. Ever. And not because there was anything wrong with him. Simply because he wasn't Jeb.

"You hate me." He sounded dejected, like she'd hurt his feelings when she hadn't even said anything.

"No. I'm just focused on other things. I have work and school, and I don't have time for anything else."

Although if Jeb asked her to do something else, she would. She totally would.

Brad walked down the hall with her, then cut off when they reached his classroom, giving her a little wave and saying he'd see her in Spanish class.

She'd probably notice him now that she'd talked to him, and she waved back, smiling her friendly smile and letting him know that she'd see him there.

School always seemed to drag after she came back from the nursing home; she had been released from prison and was back incarcerated again.

But the last bell finally rang, and she was free to drive to the farm.

As she walked from her car to the milk house with her small bag of clothes slung over her shoulder and carrying her boots, she saw what looked like blood on the stones in front of the milk house.

It seemed odd, and she tilted her head slightly, trying to figure out if something red had spilled.

She couldn't think of anything that would be in that spot and look like blood. It definitely looked like blood.

Was Jeb okay?

She changed her clothes in record time, not that it ever took her that long, especially since the milk house was heated, but not to typical room temperature standards, just warm enough so the lines didn't freeze.

Every once in a while, on the coldest days of the year, she'd stand in front of the space heater for just a few minutes, trying to get warm again before she went back out in the cold.

She made sure she was completely dressed before she came out from behind the tank, because she knew Jeb would be very embarrassed to find her in anything less than complete attire.

Not that she wouldn't be embarrassed, it was just she knew she could laugh it off. She was pretty sure Jeb's cheeks would combust, and he would probably melt into a puddle on the ground.

She would hate to have that kind of mess to clean up, plus she didn't want to make him uncomfortable. If there was anyone she wanted to be considerate to, it was Jeb.

He never was anywhere near the milk house when she came, so she went straight through the stable out the other side and into the freestall area.

He looked up in surprise as she walked in. If she didn't know better, she'd think he looked guilty. Normally he cleaned the freestalls pretty often, but he hadn't been cleaning.

She couldn't believe the relief that cooled her insides as her whole body relaxed after she'd looked him over twice and seen no bandages or wounds of any kind.

"Hey. It looked like there was blood out in front of the milk house, and I was afraid that maybe something had happened, and... I didn't know." She cleared her throat. "I was worried about you."

"I'm fine."

He didn't say anything more, which wasn't entirely unusual, so Lark went back in to feed the calves before realizing that she never started the sanitizer, so she ran back to do that, then went back to the calves.

If Jeb noticed her flub, he didn't say anything.

They always had a little bit of milk they stripped out of the cows before they put the milkers on, just to make sure that they didn't have mastitis. They had a cat pan they emptied it into just outside the parlor door, and she'd walked it out and emptied it three times before she finally came in again and said, "Polly isn't here. That's unusual. Hasn't it been about a week since she had her kittens?"

They actually hadn't seen Polly's kittens. They just assumed she had them since she was massively pregnant, and then she wasn't.

Jeb said they were probably in the hayloft somewhere, but he didn't know for sure.

None of the cats were his. Like typical farms, they were all descended from cats people had dropped off and left.

Jeb had a couple of them fixed, but it was expensive to have that done, and he wasn't exactly rolling in extra money.

Lark had paid to fix some herself, but Polly had been pregnant when she'd taken her in and the vet had refused to do her. They wouldn't do them after a certain gestation point, because the vet explained that it was too likely that they would hit an artery and Polly would bleed out.

She didn't want to kill Polly, she just wanted to fix her, so she brought her home, and they'd been resigned to having kittens.

Actually, Lark wasn't resigned, she was excited, even though she knew that that would just be more cats that would need to be fixed, if they didn't get pregnant by the time they were six months old.

Jeb pressed his lips tight together and turned away from her to finish washing a cow.

She narrowed her eyes but set the strip cup down and went to wash the cow behind his.

"I know that there are a lot of things you don't tell me," she said, being very, very understated. "But I think you're hiding something about Polly from me. Did you find her kittens? Were they dead?"

Chapter 11

"**N**o." Jeb straightened. He stood for a minute with the wash towel in his hand, the way he did when he was going to say something that was hard. Finally, he spoke. "Polly is dead. The milk truck ran over her this morning. I...got rid of her body. I...didn't think to cover up the blood, because I wanted to find the kittens. I...figured it was going to be pretty hard, and it was."

She tried to picture Jeb, climbing around the hayloft, calling for Polly's kittens. It should have been hard to picture, but it wasn't because that was just the kind of man Jeb was.

"I couldn't stand to think of them up there by themselves, scared and hungry. So, I didn't get any of my other work done, but I had just found them, when you showed up."

"Were they okay?"

"There are four of them, all four different colors, and they were fine. They were sleeping, so I thought I would come down, get the work done, and then see if I could feed them."

"You weren't going to tell me?"

"Not until tomorrow. I didn't want to get your hopes up, if...if they don't make it through the night. I figure if they're eating by morning, then they'll probably be okay."

"You're not sure they're going to eat?"

"Yeah. They've been eating from their mom, and with calves, it's kind of hard to get them to take a bottle after they've eaten from their mom. It's just not the same."

"I know." They'd both dealt with calves who'd lost their moms. Not too often. But Lark understood what he meant.

After that, she felt like the milking would never be done, which was funny, because normally she loved it and never was anxious for it to be over.

But, true to his word, as they walked out of the milk house that evening, they turned together and went around the corner of the barn, toward where they had the hay from the summer stored.

Lark loved going in the mow. Loved the way it smelled, loved the memories that were associated with it, even when it was cold, she could remember the hot days of summer, and standing in the mow stacking the hay, sitting down for a moment drinking some sweet tea, and then getting back up and going back to work.

It was fun, hard work but work she loved. She hadn't been joking when she told Jeb it was the best summer of her life.

She followed Jeb as he climbed to the highest part of the mow, back to the very back, around a couple of bales in the back and one that had broken. No one had bothered to throw the rest of the pieces down, knowing they would just crumble into bits. Around that, in a hole made by two other bales, Jeb knelt down and pointed toward the hole.

"You can look if you want to. You might need the flashlight from your phone."

"How did you ever find this?" she asked, thinking that the top of the mow behind a broken bale of hay, between two other bales, was the very last place she would ever look.

"Took me five hours."

She froze. Five hours? Of course it was true. Jeb didn't lie. It was just hard to believe that he had spent five hours looking for a litter of kittens.

Her heart swelled. That was the kind of man he was. The kind of man who couldn't allow a litter of helpless kittens to die without trying to save them, no matter how busy he was, no matter how much work there was, he'd spend five hours searching.

And then she realized that he had to dispose of Polly's body.

"Are you okay?" she asked, kneeling in front of him, forgetting about the kittens for the moment. She wouldn't have wanted to have been the one finding Polly and doing something with her.

"Fine." He looked a little confused, but his chin also jutted out, and a small muscle twitched there. It made her think that maybe he wasn't fine.

"You found Polly and took care of her by yourself?"

He lifted a slow shoulder. "You know animals die all the time. That's not the first animal I've had to do something with, that's not going to be the last." He lifted his brows a little, looking young, innocent, and a little life-weary, if that was a thing. Like sometimes all the hard things that he had to do just added on and felt like too much.

She didn't even see death as much as he did. Especially over the last nine months that she'd been in school. In the summer, they had one cow die, and they lost two calves.

Plus, his dog, Buster, had been getting slower and slower, and she figured that it wasn't going to be long until they lost him too.

Hopefully not now, not when they just lost Polly.

"I'm sorry I wasn't here. That would have been a hard thing to do."

Then a terrible thought struck her.

"Did you see the truck run over her?" Her heart leaped into her throat.

"I saw her a half a second before the tire..." His jaw clenched, and he shook his head. "I couldn't stop the truck, couldn't reach Polly."

He shrugged and looked down, probably trying to make it seem like it wasn't a big deal, but she could feel the pain. See the pinched look on his face, the deep lines around his eyes, and the clenching of his fingers.

She put a hand on his forearm, but she didn't say anything. What was there to say? She couldn't bring Polly back; she couldn't assure him that they weren't going to lose the kittens.

She'd never raised kittens at all, let alone ones as young as these would be.

"Lark..." His eyes met hers, and they knelt in the hay and stared at each other for what felt like a long moment of time.

Her realizing that he had tried to spare her the pain he felt and wishing that there had been something she could do.

He was the one who broke eye contact first. "If you want to take the kittens home, you can."

She smiled a little, knowing he said that because he knew her, knew that she loved the animals, loved taking care of them, loved the feeling of helping, just loved the cuddles and the soft fur and the idea that she could make a difference.

"All right. I have the heating pad there from the pig, though I think I'll need a bottle, and I don't have any milk replacer."

"My mom had some in the kitchen. You can come in before you leave tonight, and I'll get it out for you."

She hadn't been in his house except to get milk replacer. Hadn't touched him before tonight. She'd done what she said she was going to do, except, when someone was grieving, when someone was sad, they craved human contact. It was a natural thing.

She squeezed his forearm, and somehow, his arm moved just a little, so her hand slid down to his wrist, then their fingers entwined, and his big hand clasped hers.

Her eyes had been downcast, and now they just lifted and slid to the side just a little, looking at his hand holding hers.

Something curled in her stomach. She was tempted to put a hand there, but she didn't want to move, didn't want to break the spell, didn't want to do anything that would make Jeb think he needed to move, to take his hand away, to back up, and put the distance between them that he usually kept.

His breath seemed shallow and fast, and just as unsteady as hers.

She wasn't sure how long they stayed like that, not nearly long enough, but a small "meow" interrupted them.

Jeb's jaw tightened, and his mouth opened, then closed. Then, he looked at her and slowly pulled his hand away, watching her face.

He didn't say anything. She didn't either. Which was usual for him and unusual for her.

She wanted to ask why. Why he felt like he couldn't hold her hand any longer. It wasn't like they were somewhere where anyone was going to see them, and it wasn't like she wasn't enjoying it.

Did that mean he wasn't?

But she knew he wouldn't care whether they were somewhere where no one could see them or not. Just the idea that he was holding her hand, that he shouldn't be, would be enough. She could almost hear him saying, *God would see.*

She supposed that was all that mattered. It didn't matter whether her mom saw or someone else, whether they got told on or not. The thing that mattered is what God knew.

And God already knew deep in her heart, Lark wanted to do a lot more than just hold Jeb's hand.

"You want to reach in?" he asked with a voice that was a little husky.

She nodded. Not looking at him, a little embarrassed. After all, she told him she wouldn't touch him, and...she had.

"It's not like you to be quiet," he said while she reached her hand slowly into the hole between the bottom of the hay bales.

"I promised."

"What did you promise?" he asked immediately.

"I said I wouldn't touch you."

She felt a kitten, soft and wiggling, and so furry she couldn't tell whether she held it at the front end or the back end. So, she slid her fingers under the chubby little belly and pulled the wiggling body out. It protested with loud meows, and she smiled as she saw she'd gotten the orange one.

"I forgot about that. You...did what you said you were going to do. I mostly meant until you...were older, although it's still not a good idea."

"Are you saying the promise is expired?" she asked, not looking at him but reaching into the hole again, feeling another wiggling body.

Glancing over, her heart lodged in her chest as she saw the tiny, helpless kitten struggling in Jeb's big hand.

She wasn't sure she'd ever seen anything more appealing in her entire life. She wanted to close her hands over his, hold the kitten together, save it together.

"Here's another one." That time, when she set the kitten in his hand, she laid her cupped hand inside of his, then slowly turned it so the kitten rolled out as the back of her hand slid along the palm of his.

"Lark." He drew her name out, and there was a warning in his tone. But there was a husky note there too, which made Lark's heart flutter and her breath stumble and tingles spread from the base of her spine to the tips of her toes.

She kept her hand cradled in his, even though there was no longer a kitten in it, even though she heard the warning in his tone.

She ignored it.

The way he looked at her, the heat in his gaze, the tenderness, the admiration, she didn't want it to ever end. It made her heart feel hot and cold and jumbled up like her brains were mush and her body couldn't figure out what to do.

It was an odd feeling but a good one too. And it made her want to lean closer. So she did.

Maybe it was her imagination that he moved closer too. It could have been, because if he did, it was just a tiny bit, but it was enough to encourage her that even with the warning he'd issued, he wanted...she wasn't quite sure what. She just knew she wasn't nearly close enough to him.

She leaned forward a little more, lifting her eyes from the cute kittens snuggled down in the warmth of his hand, far enough to look at his lips.

Smooth and straight and not smiling.

She didn't look any further, but she did lean forward even more, close enough so that there was just a whisper separating them, and then—

"Lark!"

She jerked back.

Her hand flying to her throat, mostly because the sound of her brother Clay's voice scared her to death.

"I'm here!" she said, although her voice didn't sound like her own. It sounded squeaky and breathy and was filled with more disappointment than she wanted to admit. She cleared her throat and tried again. "Clay. We're up here in the hayloft getting kittens. Their mother was run over by the milk truck today."

She didn't want to meet Jeb's eyes. Surely he knew what she had been about to do. It had been more than obvious.

But with her hand on the hay bale to balance herself as she stood up, she forced herself to meet his eyes.

He was watching her. Silent. Serious. The kittens still cradled in his hand, his mouth still closed. Still not smiling.

She wanted to apologize. To tell him...she wasn't sure what. Why would she apologize? What was she telling him? That she was sorry she didn't actually get to kiss him, and she wanted to try again some other time?

That would be the truth.

"You're up in the hayloft?" Clay's voice sounded closer this time, as though he were standing at the bottom looking up.

She went out from behind the hay bales and walked over to the edge until she could see her brother. "Yeah. Did you hear me? The milk truck ran over a mama cat today. Jeb looked until he found the kittens, and we need to do something with them, because they'll die if we don't."

"I thought you were supposed to be milking cows?"

Clay's voice echoed in the big barn area. There was no accusation, but there was a deep and burning question, one that Lark couldn't really answer.

If she was supposed to be milking cows, what was she doing in the hayloft? With Jeb.

Those last two words were implied but were probably louder than the question itself.

But Clay didn't look at her like he was judging her, and he didn't look angry either.

"I should have gotten the kittens by myself. But Lark loves animals, particularly babies. She's...good at saving things."

Three sentences in a row, and a compliment on top of that.

Lark's eyes grew big, and her head whirled around to see Jeb standing just a little behind and to the side of her.

He wasn't standing in a possessive manner. In fact, the distance between them was a little too much, even for a casual stance. It made a statement.

She appreciated the statement made, except...she wished it weren't necessary. Didn't want to admit that it probably *was* necessary, and she was disappointed.

She swallowed the disappointment, turning back around to her brother. "Jeb's right. I want to be a vet. Animals... They're my thing."

Clay nodded. "I know. Why don't you come on down here, and I'll give Jeb a hand with the kittens."

It wasn't really a suggestion, although it was phrased as one.

Clay was her oldest brother. He was used to being the head of the house. He'd slid into his dad's chair at the head of the table when their dad had died, and over the years, he'd taken his job of being the eldest brother seriously.

He still deferred to their mother, of course, and she made all the decisions, but their mother had relied on him as he grew older. Now, he owned a harvesting crew of his own and commanded that the same way he'd commanded their family. Quietly, with a firm hand and a deep and abiding reliance on the Lord.

She looked up to her brother Clay and loved him with all her heart and soul.

The little bit of displeasure she read on his face cut deeper than if he would have yelled at her, insulted her, or told her that she was doing something very foolish.

For some reason, she wanted to cry as she climbed down from the hayloft and went over to Clay.

"We have two."

"I saw there were some in his hand. I'll go up and help him with the rest. You go on out to my truck. We had someone cancel on us, and the whole crew is in town for tonight. We thought we'd go to the diner for supper. Mom said you're usually home a lot earlier."

"She's right."

Lark looked down at the ground. She hadn't done anything wrong.

She had been about to do something that she shouldn't have done, but she hadn't done it.

But only because Clay interrupted her.

Still, she couldn't leave without at least trying to make things easier for Jeb. Whatever Clay was going to do, he obviously didn't want her to hear, and she didn't want Clay to give Jeb a hard time. He hadn't done anything wrong, and he hadn't been about to. Plus, she was afraid that Clay would tell him that she could no longer work there, and she didn't want that to happen.

"I wasn't doing anything wrong, I promise." She spoke low enough that her voice wouldn't carry up to the hayloft.

"I never said you were. I'll talk to you in a bit. Now go on out to the truck."

She nodded, lifting her chin up, but her normal smile was nowhere to be found.

Chapter 12

Jeb stood at the edge of the hayloft, making sure Clay didn't give Lark a hard time. They said a few low words together, words that Jeb couldn't hear, before Lark walked slowly out of the barn, looking as sad and dejected as he'd ever seen her, while Clay looked up and then grinned.

"It's been a while since I've been a monkey in a hayloft. Were these things put in tight?" he asked, referring to the hay bales. "Or am I gonna bring the whole thing down once I'm halfway up?"

"Lark and I did it this summer. Guess they're as sturdy as they can be."

Clay didn't seem upset, and it didn't feel like he was coming up to give Jeb a hard time. But why else would he be coming?

Jeb could kick himself over and over again. He'd known when Lark started working for him that he was attracted to her, even though she was way too young for him. Sure, she'd turned sixteen, but he'd looked it up.

The age of consent in North Dakota was eighteen.

Lark had two more years before it would be okay in the eyes of the law for him to do anything other than look at her.

She was just so...beautiful. Not necessarily with physical beauty, but her heart, her soul, her smile, and her infectious laugh. The way she waited for him to talk or just filled in the silence with words. Where she didn't get impatient with him, didn't act like there was something wrong with his brain just because he didn't talk the way everyone else did.

Her compassion, her love for birds, how she stood at the parlor window and laughed at the antics at the birdfeeder he'd put up just for her. How she eagerly looked forward to the birds who would be nesting in the birdhouse he'd made for her. Her delight in that simple gift.

How she put her heart and soul into saving the calves that she nursed. Her sorrow, deep and real, when they died. The way she picked herself up, lifted her chin, determined to go on with life, and didn't allow the setbacks to get her down.

She was such a sweet contradiction of tough and tender, laid-back and determined, sweet and stern. She knew how to work hard, but she wasn't brassy the way some farm girls got. She was just...perfect.

No one could blame him for working beside her day in and day out and...dreaming about her at night.

Still, being in the hayloft with her had been a bad idea, and allowing her to touch him had been even worse. But not moving away when he knew she was leaning in to kiss him had been his biggest mistake.

It was sad that his biggest regret was that she hadn't actually done it.

It could land him in jail, and here he was, not even caring.

By the time Clay made it up to the top of the hayloft, Jeb had already gone back behind the hay bales and carefully got the other two kittens out.

He stepped around the bales just in time to see Clay's head pop up over the edge before he pulled himself up.

"How many are there?" Clay asked as he stood up, brushing himself off before walking over the bales carefully, watching for the cracks, with the foresight of someone who knew that it didn't matter how tight they were packed, one could still fall through the cracks.

"Four."

Clay nodded, looking at them and even bringing one finger up and touching the white one, then the gray one. The orange and black ones were still sound asleep in his hands, and the other two had settled down with their siblings with only an occasional meow.

"You're right. Lark is going to fall in love with these," Clay muttered with a fatalistic note in his voice.

Jeb didn't say anything. Clay was right, so he just nodded.

"She loves it here." Clay looked up from the cats, looked at Jeb. "She loves animals. She is always begging Mom to have more. She wanted our dog to have puppies, she even tried to hatch snake eggs that she found somewhere. We've had toads and frogs, but mostly it's warm-blooded stuff, thank goodness." Clay shook his head. "Most of the time, she has our house looking like a zoo. I always thought it would get better as she got older, but it's actually gotten worse. Thanks to you, she had a pig in it last summer."

Jeb lifted his shoulder. "She saved it."

"I know. She wanted to get a leash for it and make it a permanent spot in the kitchen, and I told Mom we gotta draw the line somewhere, man."

Jeb grunted, but that was it.

"Anyway, she's in heaven here with all the cows, especially with the calves. She can spend an entire hour at the supper table just going on about what calves are eating what and how she's teaching some of them to bottle-feed and how one spilled the bucket..."

His voice trailed off, an affectionate smile on his face. But he lifted a hand and rubbed the back of his neck. "You know, the thing is, if you listen to Lark, she talks a lot about the animals, but at the same time, it's Jeb this and Jeb that. Jeb has all this patience, and Jeb fixed this for me, and Jeb got that for me, and I'm sure if I hadn't come here tonight, she'd be telling us at the diner how Jeb had climbed the loft and saved the lives of four kittens."

Clay didn't seem upset about it, and he didn't even say it like he thought Jeb didn't know, like somehow Jeb did know.

The truth was, he had no idea that Lark talked about him when he wasn't around. None. He especially didn't know that she went on and on about him.

Should he apologize?

"I think she has her whole family thinking you hung the moon and stars or at least you were right there beside the Lord when He hung the moon and stars. Maybe you gave advice on that too."

Jeb shook his head. "Not even close."

"I know. I know you're human, just like us. You're not perfect, but when Lark looks at you, that's what she sees. Perfection."

If Clay was trying to warn him away from Lark, that wasn't working. That made Jeb's heart do a little song and dance, and it made his lips want to quirk up in a smile.

He steeled himself, because Clay didn't come up here to lavish compliments on him. He would bet the farm on that.

Clay hooked his hand around his neck and looked up at the rafters of the barn, as though he were thinking. "You know we lost our dad when Lark was just little. She doesn't have any memories of him at all."

"I didn't know."

"I guess it doesn't surprise me. Lark talks about a lot of stuff, but she doesn't really talk about Dad, because she didn't really know him." He rubbed the back of his neck, then dropped his hand. "I'm really the only dad she knows."

Jeb was quiet.

"I don't know why. Half the time, I have no idea what I'm doing with my own life, let alone to have somebody looking at me thinking I can tell them what to do with theirs."

He put a hand over the pocket of his shirt, where a small pencil and a blue notebook stuck up, like it was there for him to jot down ideas anytime he thought of them. He touched it like it was something he normally did, grabbed it to write a few lines once in a while.

"Lark really hasn't needed a whole lot of advice though. Just a little nudge in the right direction once in a while. She was always a good kid." He shook his head. "I don't want to keep you. I could talk all night about Lark's childhood. She was a joy. She was a joy then, just as she's a joy now. But..." And now Clay's eyes got serious, and he drilled his gaze into Jeb's. "She's just sixteen."

Jeb's gaze didn't waver. Clay wasn't telling him anything he didn't know.

"The age of consent in North Dakota is eighteen. That's probably a good thing for you to remember."

Jeb didn't move for long seconds as he and Clay stared at each other. He didn't detect any threat in Clay's voice, and he also didn't detect any animosity or dislike.

"She wants to be a vet after that. Two years until she's eighteen, seven, maybe eight years or more until she's done with school and ready to do what she wants to do with her life."

Jeb nodded slowly. He knew that too. He'd said those very things to Lark more than once.

"I'd like to see her reach for the stars. It would make her mom pretty proud if she could call one of her children 'doctor.'"

Jeb's jaw clenched, and he could feel the muscle in his cheek twitch. He wanted to tell Clay that it was his goal to see that as well. But he didn't. It would sound stupid, even though it was true.

"Lark loves it here, and she's always been trustworthy. And I think you're a good man."

Clay paused as though letting that sink in. He wasn't just saying it. He believed it.

Then he continued. "I'm not going to tell her she can't come back. I'm just going to depend on the fact that I know you want the best for her. And I know you know what the best is."

Maybe Clay would have demanded his agreement. But he didn't have to demand it. Jeb agreed. That's what he wanted too. He needed to say so.

"I'll make sure she graduates and goes to college. She was born to be a vet." He didn't make promises lightly, and particularly after what had almost happened just a few moments ago—what he wanted to have happen and how disappointment still made his stomach feel dizzy—he didn't make this one lightly either. It would be a sacrifice for him to try to get Lark to do anything other than step into his arms and stay there forever.

Clay nodded his head and then said, "I can see you're a man of your word. And it's not hard to tell you care for Lark, a lot, and want the very best for her."

Obviously, Clay could see that Jeb was hopelessly, completely, and infinitely in love with Lark. What man could spend the time with her that he had and not fall for her with his whole soul? But his character demanded that he live his love by doing the best for her, no matter the cost to himself.

Clay shoved a hand in his pocket. "Maybe we'll see you around. You're always welcome at any family functions we have. There's already so many of us, one more doesn't make a difference at all."

Jeb jerked his head back; he wasn't expecting that. Of course, Clay hadn't done anything he'd been expecting. He'd compliment-ed him and then trusted him. Maybe he wasn't joking when he'd said that Lark had convinced the entire family that he was a man of character and principle.

Clay started walking. When he reached the edge, before he bent down to start down, he turned around and said, "I'm going to take Lark with me, but I'll bring her back when we're done eating. She can pick up the kittens then and ride the four-wheeler home, or I guess if you need to, or if it's too cold, you can take her home."

Jeb tried not to let his surprise show on his face. He was basically telling Jeb that he trusted him with his sister, even to the point of taking her home late at night in his truck. To the point of having her at his house long after dark.

It was the kind of responsibility that weighed hard on a man's heart, because what he wanted for Lark was every good thing. Because she represented every good thing to him. Sometimes though, having every good thing for someone else meant that the person who wanted it for them had to step back.

Jeb couldn't remember the last time he cried. He'd stood stoic at the head of his father's casket then stood the same at the head of his mother's casket, and didn't shed a tear.

But his eyes pricked now. Because Clay didn't have to tell him that what happened tonight could never, ever happen again. Not for ten long years at least, and maybe even longer. Maybe never.

If Jeb wanted the best for Lark, that was the sacrifice he had to make.

Allow her to step forward while he moved back. Stand behind her and support her, pointing her in the right direction, lifting her to the things that she was meant to do, while he took the spotlight off himself.

Did he have the character to do that? Especially if she continued to work here with him?

He hoped so.

Chapter 13

"What did you say to him?" Lark said, the second Clay got in the truck and shut the door.

"Complimented him on how cute his kittens were. What else?"

"Clay. Normally you don't mess with me."

Her brother started his pickup, backing up, turning, and pulling out of the lane. "I'm not messing with you. They're adorable."

"Clay, I know you don't care about the kittens. What did you say?"

"What were you doing?" He looked across the seat at her, his eyes holding hurt but no anger, no censure, no judgment. He turned back and looked forward through the windshield. "You don't have to tell me. You don't know all the bad things I've ever done."

"You never do anything bad." She tried not to resent it, but it seemed that way. Some people were just born perfect. Of course, she couldn't complain. Normally, she didn't have too much trouble with temptation to do things that weren't right. The biggest temptation she had was Jeb. And she hadn't even realized what a temptation he was until tonight. She still wanted to go back and finish what she started. If he didn't hate her after talking to her brother.

"See? I told you. You don't know." He grinned at her, but she didn't return his smile. She'd never felt less like smiling in her entire life.

"Are you going to tell me?"

Clay turned back toward the front, sighing, as his hands gripped the steering wheel. "I told him I trusted him. I trust you too. I told him after we were done eating, I'd bring you back, drop you off, and you can go into his house, get the kittens, and if he has any bottles or anything for you, you could pick that up too and bring them home tonight. I know you'll be in your glory with babies to raise."

She couldn't believe it. That's really what he'd said? "Really?"

He was going to take her back? He was going to just drop her off at Jeb's house? Did he think that they had done nothing wrong? Did he believe her?

"But I also told Jeb that...well, there were two things. The first is pretty serious, and you need to listen up." Clay looked over at her. He very seldom used that tone. It was his strict, *I'm not taking any nonsense about this* kind of tone. The one he usually reserved just for her brothers. "The age of consent in North Dakota's eighteen. You're sixteen. If Jeb does anything other than look at you, he could end up in jail. I know you don't want that."

"No. Of course not." She should have looked it up. But she hadn't realized until tonight how badly she wanted to do more than just look at Jeb. She *still* wanted to do more than just look at him.

"I know you think really highly of Jeb. You talk about him all the time, and it's always in a good way. He's always doing something to help you, something to make you smile, something kind, something compassionate. He works hard, and you admire that, and I do too. I think he's an honest, upright man. If something were to happen between the two of you, anything beyond you looking at him, he could end up in jail. I know you don't want that. So what you need to do is to make sure that nothing else happens."

"Nothing has happened to begin with," she said, and she didn't mean to say it stridently, but she wanted to say it with enough force that he believed her.

"All right. You've never lied to me, Lark. I don't think you're starting tonight. I believe you. But I think I'd be foolish to think that it's not possible for anything to happen. You don't have two people up in a loft looking for kittens, who don't both want to be there."

Lark looked down at her lap. She wasn't quite sure whether she was happy about that or not. What Clay was saying was that Jeb wanted to be in the loft with her. She wanted to say of course he didn't, that's where the kittens were, but Clay seemed to be insinuating something else.

"But on your side, the problems are a little different. You're not going to go to jail for anything, it's just him taking that risk. But you have two more years of high school. And you've always said, since you were able to talk, that you wanted to be a veterinarian. That's going to be a lot of hard work and study, four years of college, and another three or four years at vet school. That means you've got ten years ahead of you before you've done this thing you've wanted all your life. I just told Jeb that if he wants the best for you, the very best, he needs to step back."

Lark kept her mouth closed.

Clay had asked Jeb to stay away from her. Basically. He didn't say that exactly, but he was preying on Jeb's conscience, and Lark knew that would work. Jeb might not stay away from her for his sake, but she knew he would do it for hers. She knew, too, that Jeb would make whatever sacrifices were necessary in order to see her succeed. If that meant putting her ahead of himself, if that meant whatever he had to do to lift her up, even if it meant he stayed in the shadows, alone, he would do it.

That was just the kind of man he was. She didn't need Clay to tell her that, although she probably should thank Clay for being able to see it. To know that Jeb didn't need him to beat him up or anything like that, anything that a normal brother might do, he just needed to be reminded that he needed to live his values. To be the man he already was.

"I knew I could say that to Jeb, because you wouldn't like him as much as you do if he wasn't a man of integrity and character. Of humility and generosity. I can't see you falling for anyone who wasn't just as close to perfect as what I think Jeb probably is. Too bad he's quiet and shy, because I don't think there's a whole lot of people who quite know exactly what you know." Her brother grunted. "I supposed that's kudos to you for not being so wrapped up in yourself that you couldn't see what was under the surface, the quiet stillness that shows when people look at Jeb. But it's also a huge nod to him, because there aren't a whole lot of men around with character like his."

Clay seemed to be complimenting both of them, at the same time he was telling her she couldn't have what she wanted, Jeb.

"You know, I really do want to be a vet. But we don't have the money for college. I don't know where I'm going to get it. I mean, I know I can borrow it, but I don't want to start my life out hundreds of thousands of dollars in debt. Hoping that someday the government will forgive my debt or that it will magically disappear. I don't want that. I don't want the government, which is basically other hardworking Americans, to have to pay for me to get an education, and I don't want to start my life that deep in debt. So, being a vet might not be in the cards for me. Did you ever think that?"

Maybe she said that because she didn't know what to say about what Clay had said about Jeb. About his character and his integrity, his compassion and his loyalty, and Clay didn't even go into all the things that made up Jeb. All of the things that she...loved about him.

But Clay was right, it was his character and his integrity, his patience and his loyalty, his work ethic, and maybe it was even part of the adoration she saw when he looked at her. That a man like him could look at her and see something worth adoring. Something worth admiring.

Of course she was falling in love with him. How could she not?

She didn't care about what the rest of the world said.

"You know, sometimes you just have to have faith. It wasn't in God's plan for me to go to college. I know I'm walking exactly the path that He wants me to. And I guess that's what you need to focus on. If it's God's will for you to go to vet school, or even college, He will provide a way. But you have to have the faith that He's going to do it."

"Sometimes I'm not even sure I want to. I would be happy just milking cows for the rest of my life." She knew it. She absolutely would.

"Sometimes life isn't about what we think makes us happy. It's about living for God, doing what He wants. That might not look like the way that's going to make you happy, but it's going to be the way that's going to bring you the biggest joy and the best blessings, bar none."

She couldn't argue with that, because she knew he was right. So she didn't even try. But she did know this, "Sometimes the biggest joy and the best blessings and God's will are not where you think they're going to be. And God isn't going to tell someone else what His will for my life is. He's going to tell me."

"And I'm just going to have to trust that you are truly going to be open to God's will for your life. I know it's easy to assume that what you want is what He wants, too. You know there's a difference."

"I know. And sometimes it's hard to admit, because I think that God's going to send me to a cannibalistic tribe where there is no electricity and no running water to be a missionary for the rest of my life. I say I'll do whatever He wants me to do, but...truly I want that. Whatever it is that God wants for me. And I know it might not be what I want, but I also know that God has already equipped me to do what He wants me to do, and that will include my interest in animals and my love of farming. He's not going to put me in New York City."

"Thank goodness," Clay said with a bit of uncharacteristic sarcasm.

"Amen."

"Now that we have that settled, we can move on to other less important things."

"Don't even try to pretend that you wouldn't support me a hundred percent if God calls me to New York City."

"You know I would. But I'd worry a lot more about your safety there than I'm worried about it on Jeb's farm. He's a good man."

"You keep saying that, then you keep saying that I can't have him."

"No. I didn't say that. Don't say I did. I didn't say you couldn't have him. I just said that if you're going to be a vet, it's going to be a long time. Ten years. And I also said that for the next two years, if you care about him at all, you're not going to let yourself have him. Because he could end up in a lot of trouble, and I really hope that you're not that selfish."

"It kind of hurts my feelings that you would even suggest I might be."

"So you never did tell me what happened tonight."

Right there, any self-righteousness she felt deflated like a balloon that had been popped.

"We really did just go up to get the kittens. I put one in his lap, in his hand, and he didn't move when I leaned forward. But all I touched was his hand, and I did not kiss him."

"But you wanted to."

"I want to do a lot of things. I want to go to Alaska. I want to speak Chinese. I want to find someone for Mom who deserves her so that she can spend the rest of her life with a partner who will ease her load and make her laugh, especially since she's already spent so much of it alone. But we don't always get what we want."

"Well said," Clay said as they pulled into a spot down the street from the diner. "But you know what?" He looked over at her and smiled. His hands still on the wheel of his truck. The motor running. "Sometimes we do. And when we do, it's really sweet."

Chapter 14

Lark walked into the restaurant diner, and her heart swelled in her chest to see most of her family there. Her mom, with four of her six brothers. Plus, her sister Charlie, who met her at the door.

"Lark! What took you guys so long?"

Lark wasn't sure how to answer that. She wanted to say something about the kittens, since that was the reason she was late to begin with.

She didn't have to answer right away as Charlie put her arm around her and said, "Come on. Let's go to the restroom, and you can tell me everything."

"There might not be anything to tell," Lark said as she was being dragged by her elbow to the restrooms, with Charlie waving at the brothers and telling them they'd be right back out, but they were girls and they had to use the facilities.

The brothers made fun of them, of course, and told them to hurry because they were hungry and didn't want to have to wait three more days to eat.

It was always a loud crowd when the whole family was together. Eight kids were a lot, even if a couple of them weren't there.

"So tell me," Charlie said, opening the door and ushering Lark into the two-stall bathroom.

"There's nothing to tell," Lark said, looking at her little sister. She loved her, of course. Most of the time, they got along really well. After all, they were the only two girls in a family of boys, and they had to stick together. But Charlie was much younger, and Lark couldn't tell her everything. Even if she were older, Lark wasn't sure she could talk about something so close to her heart. Especially since she knew what she needed to do. She just didn't want to do it.

"There had to be something. The boys kept saying you guys were taking forever. They expected to get a call from Clay saying he had a flat tire or something."

"No flat tires. It's just, when Clay got there, Jeb and I were finished milking, but we had a cat get run over today—"

"Oh. That's terrible."

"Yeah, and she had four kittens. So we needed to find the kittens, because if we don't feed them, they'll die."

"Were you able to find them?"

She supposed she should have mentioned that Jeb spent most of the day looking for the kittens. But she didn't. That wouldn't have made things any different with Clay, and it wasn't like she had to tell every little detail. At least that's what she told herself.

"Yeah, we got them, and Clay came just as we were getting them out of the hay. So he talked to Jeb for a little bit, and he promised Jeb that when we were done here, he would drop me back off at his house, since I want to take care of them myself and Jeb is fine with that."

"Jeb really knows you. And he would know that if there were kittens to be fed, you would be the one who wanted to do it. Can I help?" She asked that last part eagerly.

"I hoped you would. It's going to be every two hours for a bit, and if someone does it by themselves, they're not going to get much sleep. If we can each do every other shift, that would make it a lot easier."

"All right. Let's do it! We're starting tonight?"

"Well, Jeb said that his mom had all the supplies to nurture kittens along, so hopefully yes. But sometimes it's a little bit hard to get an animal to take a bottle after they've been able to eat from their mom. So I don't know for sure if they're going to make it. You can't get attached until we know."

"You can say that if you want to, but we both know that both of us are going to be attached, and we're gonna cry like babies if they die."

"I know." But what else could one do? If she put her heart and soul into saving something, she couldn't not get attached. And Lark couldn't just give a halfhearted try to save an animal, she had to do everything she possibly could.

"Is that it?"

"Isn't four brand-new kittens enough?" Lark asked as she tilted her head.

"I guess so. I suppose it's a little bit romantic. But it would be more fun if something would happen to you, like you fall out of the hayloft and break your leg and Jeb has to carry you the whole way to the hospital in his strong arms." Charlie clasped her hands together and looked up into the corner of the restroom, like a heroine in an old-fashioned romance movie.

"Okay, that sounds painful for me and tiring for Jeb, and not the slightest bit romantic."

"It's romantic in movies."

"In the movies, you don't see the blood, you don't feel the pain, and you don't see the exhausting five-mile walk."

"It's actually more than five miles to get to a hospital from Jeb's farm."

"Exactly. And in the movies, you don't see that. They just have a little three-scene sequence showing them walking through different places, and then, bam, you're at the hospital. Easy-peasy."

"Where is your sense of romance and adventure?" Charlie asked, using an affected voice, before she grabbed the bathroom door and opened it, and they giggled before they walked out.

"All right. Here they are. And none of us have starved to death. It's a miracle," said Mav, the brother that was most likely to prank them, get into trouble, and then laugh his way out of it.

He was also the one that was most likely to complain. And if anyone was going to die of starvation, or at least pretend to, it would be Mav.

"My goodness, look at you, you've not even fainted on the floor," Lark said, giving Mav's shoulder a light swat before she sat down beside her mom.

Her mom had kept the seat beside her open for her, and her arms went around her, warm and comforting. "My goodness, normally you're home well before now every evening. What was wrong?"

"She didn't break her leg. And he didn't carry her to the hospital. It was very disappointing," Charlie called from two seats down from theirs.

They'd slid a table next to the booth and then put two extra chairs at the end of the table, and the whole family managed to sit down. They were used to improvising like that, since everywhere they went, they had to. The world just wasn't set up for a family who had ten children anymore.

"It sounds to me like Charlie's disappointed you didn't break your leg. If I were you, I think I'd be sleeping with a knife under your pillow," Boone said with a shiver, his eyes on the menu. He was probably determining whether he was going to eat three hamburgers or four.

All of her brothers were bottomless pits. She wasn't quite sure who was paying for the meal tonight, but it was going to be a big bill.

They didn't typically eat out much at all, but when the diner saw them coming, she was sure that they probably did a huge happy dance.

"Can I take your orders?" Miss Patty said, chewing gum loudly, her flip-flops snapping against her feet as she walked over to Mrs.

Stryker's seat. She knew they always had their mom order first, so she probably figured she might as well start there.

It took a little while for everyone to order, with a couple of her brothers changing their orders when they heard what someone else was doing.

Miss Patty snapped her gum, and then her flip-flops clapped as she walked away.

From experience, Lark knew it would take a while to get their food, with an order as big as theirs.

So she settled in, figuring that the boys would do their normal thing, talking about the weather, farming, and in between all that picking on their sisters.

She wasn't disappointed, since Mack started right away. "How old is Jeb?"

Lark didn't even get an answer out before Boone said, "You heard about him all winter. I thought it was really weird, now you're hanging out at his house until all hours of the night, and Preacher has to go get you."

"So what exactly were you guys doing?"

"I suppose you are smooching up in the hayloft," Mav said.

Lark prayed her cheeks did not get red.

"Boys. That's enough." Preacher didn't raise his voice, and he didn't sound angry, but the teasing stopped immediately.

Preacher didn't miss a beat, but he started in with the harvest crew schedule for the next week. Cord didn't go out, since he had started raising Percherons before he was even out of high school, and while he didn't make a great living with them yet, he also made handcrafted sleds and sold them online. He made enough to pay his farm payment, and he said he was building his herd.

Regardless, the rest of the boys talked about the schedule, and then the weather, and then all the things that a typical farm family discussed over dinner.

Lark missed those dinners when everyone was home and the table was full to bursting with all of her brothers.

It was a lot quieter, especially when they were out on harvest crew, since most of them still lived at home.

It wasn't the same.

It made her a little bit sad, sad to think that she was growing up, that her brothers would soon be getting married and leaving forever and she only had a few years left at home with her mom and sister, that she almost kissed a boy tonight.

Not a boy. A man.

Maybe that was why she didn't fit in with the kids at school. With a family like hers, how could she? They talked about real-world stuff, and they didn't gloss over the problems of life. They expected her to be responsible and gave her responsibilities and then didn't check up on her.

Whatever it was, the kids at school seemed immature and uninteresting when lined up against Jeb.

But Preacher was right. If she loved him, she needed to stay away from him. For his own good.

She joined in the laughter and fun of her family, and while she had a great evening, she wasn't disappointed when it was time to go. She was eager to get back to Jeb. She wanted to...talk to him.

She didn't think she could apologize. Because it would be a lie. She wasn't sorry for what she did. But she was going to try not to do anything like that again. Because while what happened tonight had not been wrong, if it happened again, they might not be interrupted.

Still, she just wanted to make sure he was okay. Even though she knew he probably was.

Or maybe she just wanted to make sure that he wasn't blaming her and wasn't angry at her. That meant more to her than anything.

Whatever it was, she climbed out of Preacher's truck gratefully, thanking him for the ride and pausing when he stared at her.

"I love you, Lark."

Preacher really knew how to make her feel guilty. How to keep her in line, too.

After all, she didn't want to disappoint or disrespect the brother who loved her and trusted her.

"I love you, too. Thanks for tonight."

She didn't mean just the meal, which Clay paid for, but she meant everything. He could have gone in, guns blazing so to speak, angry, big, and tough and threatening.

But he'd taken Jeb's measure, and he treated him like a man who deserved to be respected. She appreciated that. Even if nothing ever happened between her and Jeb. If the Lord didn't have them together in His plan later in life, she appreciated the fact that her brother was someone that she was proud of and wasn't ashamed to be seen with, and she loved to have him meet the man she was interested in.

"Be careful coming home. It's dark." He lifted his brows. "It might rain too. If Jeb needs to bring you home, you know that's okay."

She nodded. "Thanks again."

He took a deep breath and looked at her, almost as though he were thinking the same things that she had been thinking earlier. About the night, and the family, and how things used to be, and how they would never be the same again.

Maybe he was looking forward to the rest of his life, maybe he was eager to move on, since they couldn't go back so they might as well go forward. She didn't know, but she just felt a kinship with him then, something she had never had before.

"There are some mistakes in life that once you make them, you can't ever take them back. Be cautious. Those are the mistakes that you really don't want to make." With that, he nodded his head at her, and she stepped back, closing the door.

He was gone just a few seconds later, and she still stood there looking after him.

He could have said that to both her and to Jeb. The mistake she made could ruin Jeb's life. The mistake Jeb made could ruin hers.

She thought about that as she walked up the walk, where the dim light above the sink shone out the kitchen door and onto the walk.

Jeb had the door open before she even had reached the top step.

"You okay?" he asked gently, concern pouring out of his eyes.

For some reason, that caring concern caused the back of her throat to close, and her eyes to fill.

She shoved them away quickly, not wanting him to not believe her when she said she was fine. After all, if she was crying whenever she said it, she wouldn't believe herself either.

"Clay is the best man I know," she finally said. Then she grinned a little. "I know he's my brother, so my opinion is a little biased, but he's the best."

"I haven't talked to him too much before tonight, but I guess I have to agree with you. He's a good man."

"And he said that about you. That you are a good man. Of course, he said a lot of other things, that you had character and integrity and a great work ethic, and a lot of other good things," she ended lamely. After all, she could hardly say that he said that was why she liked him, because of his character and integrity.

"But?"

"But he said the same thing that you've been saying since I started here. I just need to be careful."

She looked him straight in the eye, and while he was in shadow because his back was to the light, he could probably see her face clearly. She was never any good at hiding what she felt, never any good at pretending to be something she wasn't. So he probably saw the unvarnished truth on her face. How he read that, she had no idea. But in her heart, she felt determined to do whatever it took to be the friend that Jeb deserved. The friend who protected him, honored him, and cared for him, and made sure that he lived the best life he could, the friend who did not put any stumbling blocks in front of him.

"He said you would be a really good friend. Loyal and dependable. I hope I'm the same kind of friend to you."

Jeb nodded slowly. She didn't need a lot of light to read what his face said. He cared about her. A lot. And he didn't need her brother to say anything to him in order for him to treat her the way she needed to be treated.

If anything, the tenderness in his eyes was more pronounced.

"You already have been," he finally said.

That right there made her want to cry again. She hadn't been a good friend to him. If she had, she wouldn't have been leaning toward him when Clay interrupted them. She wouldn't have nestled her hand in his and kept it there defiantly, loving how it felt.

She realized she hadn't said the most important thing Clay had told her, so she tossed her hair a little, pushed her shoulders back, and put a cheerful smile on her face, breaking the seriousness of the kitchen. "He said that I could keep working here, and that if you needed to drive me home tonight, since it was supposed to rain, and I rode the four-wheeler here since my car had to go to the shop to get the oil changed, you could."

She added those two things together, just so she didn't make a big deal about her being able to continue working there. She wasn't sure exactly what Clay had said to Jeb, but just in case it included any threats, she wanted to make sure that Jeb knew.

"This is what you want?"

She knew immediately that he was asking if she wanted to continue working there.

"Yes!" There was no hesitation whatsoever.

He pressed his lips together, almost as though he was hoping that she would say something else, and her heart sank, but then he turned.

"My mom had everything we needed to raise these kittens. Including kitten milk replacer, which was expired, but I used it anyway because they needed to eat. She also had a heating pad. I put everything in the box right here. The pad is on with the kittens on it."

She had never heard Jeb ramble, but it seemed like that's what he was doing. After all, it was four or five sentences together without a break.

As quickly as he started, he stopped, almost as though he realized that he was talking a lot more than he normally did.

"If you want to keep them here, we can? Although my sister Charlie is really looking forward to having them tonight."

Just then, a flash of lightning blinked through the kitchen, and both of them stilled and listened.

It was several seconds before the thunder cracked and boomed and rolled.

"Yes. You take them." Another flash of lightning lit up the kitchen. He waited for the thunder to fade away before he said, "I think it's best for me to take you home."

She nodded. "I can put the four-wheeler away."

"I'll do it. Do you need me to pick you up in the morning? Take you to school?"

Part of her wanted to say yes, just so he would, but she couldn't do that. Not if she wanted to keep her vow. The one where she said that she would do everything in her power to make sure that nothing happened to Jeb.

"My brothers are all home. They had a cancellation, and they decided to surprise Mom. When things get busy, we don't see them for weeks or even months on end. And since they were already in the area, they figured they'd stop in. Any one of them will take me to school and bring me here afterward."

He nodded. "I'll carry that."

He moved to unplug the heating pad, and then rolled the cord up so he held it in his hand, and then picked up the box.

She waited by the door, opening it so he stepped out on the porch as the first big, fat drops of rain started to fall.

"Hold on a second, I'll run around and open the truck door for you."

He jerked his head up, waiting for her to go around him and run down the steps in front of him.

She opened the door, then realized she needed to be sitting on the seat in order to hold the box, so she jumped in, just in time, as he came along behind her, hunched over the box to keep the worst of the rain out as he set it in her lap.

He didn't touch her at all, which disappointed her but made her happy at the same time.

"Don't forget your belt," he said before he shut the door.

She bit her lips, grabbing her belt, buckling, wishing they had the kind of relationship where he would have done it for her.

They drove in silence, her thinking and not doing her usual chatter, him quiet as usual.

Although, when they were together, he talked more, so maybe he wasn't as quiet as usual. Maybe he was quieter than usual.

But she could hardly fault him, since she was too.

She wanted to continue working for him, and she knew she would continue to be attracted to him, continue to like him. But she could control herself. She was...almost an adult, with an adult's responsibilities.

If she wanted to be treated like an adult, she had to act like one and make the mature decision. That was to make sure that her relationship with Jeb stayed on a friendship level. At least until she was eighteen. Because, unlike Clay, she was pretty sure God didn't want her to be a vet. He wanted her to be the wife of a dairy farmer in North Dakota.

Chapter 15

I t was a cold, early morning in October as Lark drove down Jeb's driveway in her car, smiling.

She was one month into her senior year, with just eight more months to go.

Less than a year until she turned eighteen. Less than a year until she could tell Jeb how she really felt. In less than a year, she could be married.

She thought about that every morning as she drove to work. Was it really work? Maybe she should say she thought of it every morning as she drove to the best job in the world. Couldn't think of anything else she'd rather do, and she definitely couldn't think of anyone else she'd rather work with.

A person would have thought that after years of working together, she'd have gotten tired, bored, or wanted to do something else, or at the very least, Jeb and she would have started to irritate each other, but she could honestly say there had never been a day she hadn't wanted to jump out of bed, even at three fifteen in the morning, and drive to work.

Considering that all she did was throw a ballcap on her head, and she often wore her dirty clothes from the night before, it was a wonder that Jeb still looked at her like he admired her and wanted to be with her.

She'd successfully stayed away from him, not touching him at all, not since the day Clay had caught them in the hayloft with the kittens.

And she had to say, she'd adjusted her mindset to convince herself that she enjoyed being friends with him. Enjoyed building a solid friendship, one where he knew that he could count on her for anything. He could call her, day or night, and she would answer right away. He could ask for anything, and she would give it to the best of her ability.

She set herself the goal of being the very best friend that Jeb ever had.

Whether or not she was succeeding, she wasn't sure, but it was her ultimate goal.

Regardless, she wasn't satisfied with herself and figured she could do better. A lot better.

With that thought, her smile deepened, because she loved the idea that she was creating a solid and enduring relationship that would last a lifetime.

Of course, the idea that Jeb had lost interest in her, or hadn't really been interested to begin with, was real, but she preferred not to dwell on that. If it turned out he wasn't, she would be heartbroken of course, but she would still have a really, really good friend.

Her smile faded slightly as the barn came into view.

In all the time that she'd worked for Jeb, she'd never beaten him to the barn.

But the lights weren't on.

Her eyes flew over the milk house, but the windows were dark, the barn was dark, nothing moved.

She slowed, searching the barn area and then looking toward the house.

Was he sick? He'd been fine last evening when she said goodbye to him and went home.

They talked about all the normal things, nothing special. It had just been a regular day. The kind she loved. She was extremely happy with regular days.

But she definitely didn't like this. This stillness. The newness. This thing that had never happened before. The barn being dark, Jeb...not around.

Could the electricity have gone out?

She tried to think as to whether or not Jeb and her farm were on the same line.

They'd gone out a couple of times in the winters, but Jeb had a generator and soon had it back on long enough to milk the cows.

Maybe the lights had gone out and his alarm hadn't gone off.

For herself, she set an alarm, but she always woke up before it went off, eager to get to work. Maybe Jeb didn't. Maybe he slept soundly and needed his alarm every morning.

Hoping that was the case, she pulled slowly into the spot where she always parked, right beside his pickup.

Her eyes went from the barn back to the house, and then she saw the shadow.

Jeb. Sitting on the steps, his forearms resting on his knees, his head looking down at the ground between his feet.

He looked...sad and dejected.

Jeb was quiet, but he was never depressed. She learned that his quirked-up lips equaled one of her huge smiles, and when one side pulled back, he found humor in something. His face was full of expressions that she'd learned to read better than she could read her own.

But she didn't have to see his face to see that his body was saying that something really, really terrible had happened.

With her heart in her throat, she pulled on her car door, for some reason slowly getting out instead of rushing to him like she wanted to.

She closed the door just hard enough for it to click, then walked around the front of her car and toward the steps.

When she'd been sitting in her car, she'd been too far away to notice. Now that she'd walked closer, she could see the still form of Buster that rested beside him on the porch.

Her hand went to her mouth, and she gasped, and without even thinking, she slid in on the other side of Jeb, her arm going around his shoulders and her head leaning down beside his, until they were cheek to cheek.

"Jeb. Oh my goodness. I'm so sorry. I... I knew he was getting older, but..."

"Yeah."

His cheek wasn't wet, his shoulders didn't shake, and his voice didn't quiver. He just sat, quiet and sad.

"He was such a good dog. So well-trained and dependable. He was always exactly where we needed him to be, and he didn't scare the cows, he just got them for us."

"Yeah."

"I know you loved him. I... I did too, but not like you. I only knew him for a little while, but he was the dog you grew up with."

She knew Buster was in his late teens, that Jeb had gotten him when Jeb was ten or so. He'd been a birthday present, after their old dog died, and Jeb had spent weeks crying over him.

Jeb laughed a little when he told the story then, but his eyes had slid to Buster, and there had been a sadness there. Like he knew the loss was coming.

That was what was so hard about love, but as humans, they couldn't not love. They couldn't protect themselves from that pain.

And if the ache in her chest was any indication, Jeb was feeling a lot of pain.

Of course, a large part of her pain was the knowledge that he hurt. That was what friendship was, when a person's friend hurt, they hurt with them. A person couldn't watch their friend suffer and not suffer too.

Of course, the fact that she was also in love with Jeb probably contributed to the deep sense of sorrow and loss she felt and the even deeper pain that made her very soul ache.

"I wish I could feel this for you. I wish I could do it so you didn't have to."

His head moved just slightly, not enough to make her feel like she needed to pull her head away, just enough to know that he was denying it.

"I wouldn't let you, wouldn't want you to, probably no more than you would want me to go through it for you."

He always knew. He just did. He was quiet, but he observed a lot, and he understood that his pain was hers.

She did not know how to help him, how to make it better, and all she could think of was that if it were her, she'd just want to sit and be miserable for a little bit. Sit and think about her friend, the times they'd had together, and maybe just have someone sit quietly beside her, knowing that they would bear her pain if they could.

So that's what she did. She kept her arm around Jeb and sat on the front porch with him, while the eastern sky lightened and day started to break.

Sometimes a person just needed someone to sit beside him and be there for them. Sometimes they just needed time to process. Sometimes they just needed to stop and figure things out.

She wasn't sure exactly what it was that Jeb needed, but whatever it was, she would be there for him, no matter how sore her butt got from sitting in the same position. Her arm had fallen asleep long ago, and she was freezing from sitting in the cold air, not moving.

"Your teeth are chattering. Go on inside."

"I'm not leaving until you do. Unless you want me to go milk the cows for you. I'll do it alone, if you just need time."

His head turned, and she drew back just a little, until they were sitting eye to eye in the brightening light of dawn. His hand reached up and settled down on hers, which she hadn't even realized was resting on his leg.

Somehow their fingers threaded together, and he said, "No. I don't want you to do it alone."

"And I don't want you to do this alone."

He seemed to understand, because he didn't say anything else about her chattering teeth or her lips which she knew had to be some shade of blue.

"He was just a good friend, that's all."

"I know."

He was quiet for a while, and he mentioned before that he kind of liked to listen to her talk, especially when he didn't know how to voice his thoughts, so she said, "I know you've been making birdhouses in the evening, and it was nice to think about you over here, with Buster beside you, so you weren't alone. I... I'll not be quite so happy now that I know he's not here to keep you company."

He often mentioned making the birdhouses in the evening, saying that he was selling them online, separate from the farm, because he was saving up to buy something.

She wasn't sure exactly what he was saving up for, and she didn't ask.

She didn't know how he ran the finances of the farm, but whatever he was doing with the birdhouses seemed like it would be something completely different from the farm, maybe a vacation he wanted, or some kind of personal item, maybe a motorcycle. She could see Jeb on a motorcycle, just taking a solo trip across the United States. She thought he would probably enjoy that, if he could ever get himself to leave the farm long enough.

She smiled at the idea.

Chapter 16

"**I** know I'm young. I've never really lost anyone." Lark sat still beside Jeb.

"Your dad," he reminded her.

"Thanks for remembering, but I don't even have any memories of him. None. At all. I see pictures, and he's just a stranger in a photo, and I don't really feel anything at all when I look at him. Other than maybe some curiosity as to what he might think of how I turned out. I don't know if he'd be proud of me, but I guess I just hope he's not disappointed."

"He's not."

His words helped reassure her, even though they were still soft and laced with grief.

"I remember my brother Wilder. He's a good bit older than me, and he left years ago. I'm not sure I was even ten. He just left. I suppose that's the closest thing I've had to losing someone in my family. Mom still cries about that sometimes. I talked to Charlie about it, and occasionally my brothers. No one can find him, he's never contacted us. I guess we just kind of think that he must have done something that would have embarrassed Mom, and he couldn't face her with it. That's all we can figure out."

"Makes sense."

"I miss him sometimes. The family just doesn't seem complete without him. You know?"

Jeb nodded his head.

"I guess that's the difference between you and me." She didn't really like to point out their differences. He already thought she was too young, and she didn't like bringing attention to that, but she went ahead as his fingers tightened around hers.

Maybe she should pull her hand away, maybe he should, but the shared grief trumped everything else, and the idea of comforting him was all she thought about.

"What is?" he prompted after she was uncharacteristically quiet for a bit.

"You lost your dad, then your mom, your sisters don't come around much, and you're alone. You realize that I'm hardly ever alone? Maybe when I'm in the car on my way to school, and half the time, I have Charlie with me. So coming here to the farm, all ten or fifteen minutes of it, is the most alone time I get some days."

"You were made to be with people."

She shook her head. "I love people, but those ten or fifteen minutes I get by myself, I cherish them. But I suppose you're right, I wouldn't want to be alone all the time. But I guess my thought was, you've already suffered a lot of loss, and I don't really know how to help you."

"I don't think there is any help for it. It's just the idea, especially with my parents, that I'd see them again. With Buster... I don't know."

She couldn't assure him of that, because she didn't know either.

"I just know death makes life worth living."

She huffed out a breath. "How so?" She hadn't really considered that.

"If you didn't feel, you wouldn't really be living. So there has to be pain. There has to be an end. Otherwise, it wouldn't be special. The time that you spend with something." He paused, a long pause, then he lifted her hand slowly and pressed his lips to her knuckles. "With someone."

Her breath hitched. She couldn't move. Couldn't breathe, couldn't feel her heartbeat, couldn't feel anything but her skin where his lips touched and the feeling like warm syrup that started there and spread throughout her entire body, the feeling that made her think everything about this moment was exactly right.

His lips stayed pressed against her for what felt like long moments but probably wasn't that long at all.

"Death makes us appreciate what we have. Makes us cherish the moments. It gives us something to live for."

"What's that?"

"Dying well. Haven't you ever thought of that?"

"No." She almost said she was only seventeen, of course she wasn't thinking about dying. She was thinking about spending the rest of her life with him, which seemed to stretch off into eternity, but he was right. She would die one day. Of course she wanted to do it well.

"How do you do that?" she asked, just because she didn't want him to move, wanted him to stay, to continue to talk, continue with his lips brushing her knuckles, with his warm body next to hers, and with his hand holding hers tight.

She was no longer cold, no longer sore, no longer anything but very, very alive. And very, very sad, because the person she loved best in the entire world was heartbroken and there was nothing she could do to help other than stay right there beside him.

"Death gives us a purpose, right?" He looked over at her, his lips brushing against her knuckles as he did. "We know it's going to happen."

She nodded, breathing in his air, their heads close together.

"It's the last thing we do here on earth."

She'd never thought of that before.

"Do we want to do it well? I mean, it's the last impression anyone will ever have of you. What do you want them to remember you as?

And taking it a little further, what do you want them to remember your life as? What do you want them to say at your funeral?"

She wanted them to say that she was his wife, but that wasn't exactly what they were talking about, and it wouldn't suit the conversation. He was talking about character. What character traits did she want people to remember her as having.

"Jeb Malone will be remembered as honest. He never said anything that wasn't true. Ever. Dependable. Loyal. A hard worker, who took care of his animals, as well as anyone could."

His lips curved just a bit, but she wasn't finished.

"Someone who loved deeply."

He glanced at Buster and then right back to her. The look he gave her felt like it singed her heart, it was so strong and true, but she forced her mouth to move.

"Someone who picked up and did what needed to be done, even when he didn't feel like it."

Their hands were joined, they were sitting close together, but they hadn't done anything wrong, and as much as she loved the position they were in, they wouldn't do anything wrong.

"Someone who would sacrifice in order for others to have what they needed."

"I could say all the same things about you. And add that you're always happy. Always have a smile, always try to find a way to make people around you smile, no matter how taciturn and serious they were."

He was talking about himself, and she smiled.

"Aren't we supposed to be talking about Buster, and the life that he had, and the things we want to remember?"

"Buster inspired this conversation. We are sitting here now, talking about how we want to be better because of him and his death. We know that."

He was right.

"Isn't that what you want your life to be too? Something that inspires others to be better? Something that makes them stop and think and say I want to change the path I'm on, I want to go on a harder, better path, a path that will make me a better person, a better Christian, a better disciple, someone who's more encouraging, more uplifting, better than what I am today?"

"Yeah. That's what I want." She had never thought of that before, but he was nudging her to have a purpose for her life. Nudging her to say, to know, to think, and not just live each day as it came, blindly doing whatever it was that felt good, but to have an endgame in mind.

She could do at least as well as a football player, couldn't she? They didn't go into a ballgame with no clue on what they were going to do.

Why would she go into life with no clue of what she was going to do? Shouldn't she start each day with an idea of what she wanted to accomplish at the end? Not winning the game, necessarily, but being an encouragement, being a blessing, and having an idea of how to get from where she was to where she wanted to be.

"Buster sparked a whole bunch of new ideas in my mind." She smiled a little, not because she wasn't still sad, but because she didn't want to be sad. She wanted to look forward not backward, and that seemed to be what Jeb was directing her to do. To use the grief and the hardness to look ahead, to change course if necessary, to dig in harder if that's what one had to do, but also to remember that death was coming, so life was precious.

"Thanks for sitting with me this morning," he said before her smile had faded away. His lips were still tilted up, and he moved his head. "Time is precious."

"Time with you is priceless," she said, her brows lifted, her eyes trying to tell him what she was trying to say, without actually saying it.

He understood, because his smile got a little bigger, and he nodded. "Same with you."

They sat there for a while. Lark lost track of time, lost track of her thoughts, as they scattered around, with death and life and cherishing each moment vying for position in her head, as well as the deep desire to comfort and to encourage and to support.

"Just because we look forward doesn't mean that endings aren't hard," Jeb finally said as he looked away, and then he lifted her knuckles to his lips one last time before he slid his fingers from hers. "I think I'll let him lie there on the porch one last morning while I go milk the cows, and you better head to school, or you're going to be late."

"I'll call Mom. I know it'll be okay. I'll stay here. I'll milk the cows with you, and I'll help you bury Buster."

He shook his head. "You can help me with the cows if your mom says it's okay, but I'll bury Buster myself."

She wasn't sure whether it was because he didn't want her to miss school, or whether it was because he wanted to have the time. Whichever, at least he was letting her help with the barn work.

They stood, and for the first morning in more than a decade and a half, Buster wasn't beside Jeb as he walked off the porch steps and out to the barn.

Lark took small comfort in the fact that Buster wasn't there, but for this morning at least, she took his place so Jeb didn't have to walk alone.

She wanted that to be their life. Her beside Jeb, so they weren't alone.

Chapter 17

"So what are you doing for Christmas?" Lark asked, putting a milker on while she spoke.

Jeb smiled in his head, but he didn't let her see that he was amused. "The same thing I said I was doing yesterday when you asked."

They'd worked together for a long time now, and he felt as comfortable with Lark as he had with his mom and dad. It was impossible not to feel comfortable with her.

Of course, he couldn't think about the things he felt with her. He'd been doing a good job of focusing on being the best friend to her that he could be. It wasn't hard. Lark was an easy person to like, an easy person to want the best for, an easy person to sacrifice for.

It was cold now, and he did all the jobs that required him to be out in the snow. He always tried to beat her out to the barn so he could get things started, to make sure the milk house was warm, to make sure that things would be easier for her.

He wasn't paying her enough to suffer, but she never complained. Not about the pay, not about the cold, not about anything.

If it was cold, she just lifted her shoulder and said at least it wasn't colder.

If it was hot, she said at least there's a breeze blowing.

It didn't matter what happened, it didn't bother her.

How could he not feel comfortable and completely at home with a person like that?

Of course, the fact that she had a beautiful heart and a sweet soul, only meant that it was easy to fall in love with her.

"All right, so I'll ask you the same thing I asked you yesterday—"

"And the day before. And the day before that. And the day before that. In fact, I think you started about two weeks before Halloween, asking me if I would go to your house and eat Christmas dinner with your family."

"Yes. And you know that story in the Bible about the child who constantly asked his father for something, and Jesus said that of course eventually his father gives it to him because he keeps asking."

"I think you might have your stories mixed up."

She shrugged, throwing her paper towel in the trash and grabbing another one. "Admit it. I'm right. Jesus said keep asking, and eventually the person you're asking will cave. Have you caved yet?" She tilted her head and gave him a considering look, like it was possible that he was going to say yes today, when he had said no for the last sixty-odd days.

"No," he said easily, walking over to the second cow in line, picking up the milker she had just kicked off, flipping it over, and sticking it back on her with four slurps of air.

"How about now?" She gave him an engaging grin, one that took every ounce of his willpower to resist.

"No."

There was no way he was going to her house, facing her brothers, hanging out with her family, like he was...someone.

He had told Clay that he would step back, that he would let her go, that he wouldn't try to hold her, when she was meant to go to college and vet school and become a veterinarian. If he showed up for Christmas dinner, Clay would think he was breaking his promise.

As much as he might want to, as much as he wanted to get to know Lark's family, because he wanted them to be his family too, he couldn't. He'd made a promise.

"All right. You've got to tell me, why?" Lark stopped with her feet planted, her little hands stuck on her hips, as she glowered at him.

He snorted but didn't laugh. She didn't scare anyone like that. She couldn't make herself look mean if she tried.

That was okay, she looked cute instead, which was nice. He wished he had a picture of her looking like that. He would be tempted to get one of the newfangled phones, just so he would have a picture of Lark to carry around with him. Not that he wanted her to know it, she couldn't, but... She was leaving. Next year this time, she would have forgotten all about him, and he would at least have a picture to remember her by.

He put another milker on, but Lark didn't move. She stood with her feet planted, her eyes on him. For once, she wasn't smiling. The times when she wasn't smiling were few and far between, and he hated them.

"Jeb."

He paused, milker in his hands, under the cow, ready.

He could tell her. He could explain why. He probably owed her that explanation anyway. Because she knew he would not normally turn her down. Not for anything. All she had to do was ask. She didn't even have to ask, she just had to say she wanted something, and he'd provide it if he could. He wasn't sure whether that was what normal friends did or not, but it was what he wanted to do. It was how he showed her that he was there for her. By actually being there, not just giving it lip service.

He put the milker on, then he straightened, walking over until he stood in front of her. Not close, just enough that she knew that he was going to talk to her, and she was listening.

It took him a minute to square around his thoughts, to make them into coherent sentences, ones that he could hopefully keep track of, and say what he needed to say, and have it make sense.

Sometimes when things were really important to him, he had a hard time keeping his train of thought, making the words come at the same time.

"I'd like to go."

That was the truth, and she recognized that, he saw the light come into her eyes, and her lips turn up.

Then her brows went down. "But?"

He bit his tongue, thinking, and then he said, "But I can't go to your house. I can't be your guest at Christmas. I can't hang out with your family, because you invited me. I can't do that, because everyone there is going to think I'm there because of you."

She took a breath. He held a hand up and her lips twitched, remembering how they used to talk, with her chattering until he put his hand up for her to stop.

"And they would be right." He pursed his lips and looked away. "You told your brother that we wouldn't do that. That there wouldn't be any claims, there wouldn't be any... any...thing." He used his hand to gesture between the two of them. "Between us. You're my friend. That's all you can be. Friends don't hang out at other friends' houses at Christmas, unless they're at college and don't have anywhere else to go. We both know that's not me."

Her mouth had slowly fallen open as he had spoken, and it turned into an O.

She jerked her head up, acknowledging his words. And then, very uncharacteristically of Lark, she turned without a word and went back to washing udders.

That was easier than he thought it was going to be. He thought he was going to have to field questions and give more excuses, and possibly admit everything that Clay and he had talked about. But she understood. She accepted it.

He saw her texting on her phone later and didn't think anything about it. It was Christmas Eve, and she probably had various last-minute things that she had to do, with a family as big as hers. Plus, everyone would be in tonight, and they would be going to church.

She'd already asked him if he was going, and he told her no, although he hadn't really decided. If he went, he'd be sitting by himself in the back. He'd done it before, and it didn't really bother him, except he would see the back of Lark's head and wish she were beside him.

And that, that was definitely not a good way to spend Christmas Eve.

He was better off staying at home, working on the birdhouses he'd been selling online and thinking about the baby in the stable and not about the woman he couldn't have.

He thought they had everything settled, and so when the door to the parlor burst open, he couldn't contain his surprise.

Lark's sister Charlie stepped down the stairs and stood facing him.

That had never happened before, and he thought that there must be some kind of emergency.

"Lark?" he said, since Lark's back was toward her sister, and she didn't seem inclined to go over and greet her.

That would leave Jeb to greet her, and Jeb wasn't exactly great at talking to people. Lark knew that, and she almost always greeted everyone who came in, male or female, friend of hers or business associate of his.

She did the talking, as much as she could, and broke the ice until he was ready to slide into the conversation.

She did it effortlessly, without him asking, without him saying, and without them ever talking about it. It was just something they did together.

But today, Lark either forgot her position or was mad at him.

Still, he recognized Charlie, because she looked so much like Lark, a little taller, a little bigger boned, a little lighter hair color, possibly, although it was covered by a beanie hat and he couldn't be sure.

"Good night, it is freezing out there."

Her cheeks were rosy, and she looked like she was an icicle.

She must have driven the four-wheeler, since she wasn't old enough to have a driver's license.

He felt trapped; to turn his back and walk away from her would be rude, but he didn't know what else to say.

"I'm Charlie, and I know you're Jeb. We've met before, but I haven't seen you for a few months." She was not quite as animated and outgoing as Lark, but she didn't seem to be shy. She walked over to him with her hand out. Rather mature for a high schooler.

He wiped his on his pant leg and then gingerly took hers. She squeezed firmly and met his eyes while she shook.

"I just talked to my mom, and she and I were hoping that you could come for Christmas dinner tomorrow as our guest."

Charlie looked smug.

Jeb's lips pursed, and he turned his head slowly to look at Lark.

Lark had her back to him still, and she was washing the same cow that she'd been washing when Charlie walked in.

None of the cows were that dirty, since the ground had frozen weeks ago, and there was no mud whatsoever for them to get into.

"Lark?" he said, low and slow with all the warning in the world in his voice.

"I'm sorry, Jeb, she didn't come to see me. She came to see you. On behalf of my mom and her guests. That's what she said anyway." Lark shrugged, like she had nothing at all to do with anything, and then went back to washing that same poor cow. She would be chapped and sore in the morning.

Jeb gritted his teeth, mostly so that he wouldn't smile, but partly because the woman was so annoying.

She wasn't even a woman. She was just a girl. But he had to admit, she had him wrapped around her fingers, and he would do whatever she wanted him to do, although he couldn't break a promise for her. But she'd arranged it so he didn't have to. She had to know that he would say yes a million times over to her sister, and her mom apparently, just so he could be there, just because she wanted him.

And he wasn't going to deny that the fact that she wanted him, that she would go to these lengths to get him, made him feel more happy and blessed from the roots of his hair the whole way to his toes and back again, filling every corner of his body in between.

He never had someone want him like this.

Slowly, he looked back at Charlie, who looked like she would wait all day for his answer, maybe because her sister had warned her that he could be slow.

"Yes."

Charlie looked at him, like she didn't quite understand, and then her eyes lit up.

"You'll come! Mom is going to be thrilled, and so am I. Thank you!" She turned on her toes and started striding back out of the parlor. Then, she stopped quickly, turned around, and said, "We eat at one. It's always a little later on Christmas. Is that okay?"

He nodded slowly.

"All right. Don't worry about bringing anything, we've got it covered."

That made his heart flip. He should bring something! It was Christmas! He couldn't show up at other people's houses without a gift. But he didn't have anything.

He couldn't exactly bring a cow. Although, he did have meat in the freezer from the last cow he had to put down. But he couldn't take that, could he?

Charlie left, and Jeb went back to working. After ten minutes had gone by without Lark saying anything, he figured for once, he would break the silence. He waited until a new set of cows had walked in, and they were washing them together before he said, "That was a neat walk-around."

She grinned at him, not the slightest bit scared that he would be upset. Of course not. She knew he worshiped the ground she walked on.

If she didn't, she had to be the most naïve person in the entire world.

"Clay didn't talk to you to scare you. My family loves you, and honestly, we always have guests for Christmas. Anyone who doesn't have somewhere else to go, who might be alone, always ends up at our house. My mom makes sure of it. It's just something we do. Although, I don't want you with us because you'd be alone. I want you there because..." Her mouth clamped closed, like maybe she'd said too much, and he supposed it was the time of year that felt romantic and special, especially for couples. It was why he didn't want to go to the Christmas Eve service. He didn't want to go alone. Didn't want to go home alone. Didn't want to be reminded that everyone had someone, except for him.

"He didn't scare me." He wanted to be clear about that. "I made a promise."

He wanted her to finish her sentence. Why she wanted him there. He wanted to prompt her about it, but they were skating on dangerous ground there. It was better if he didn't hear what she had to say. Unless she was going to say she wanted him there because he was her very good friend, but that probably wouldn't feel very good either.

He did want to be her very good friend, but he wanted to be more too.

It was just a few months until she turned eighteen, but it was seven or eight more years until she became a vet.

He had a long time to wait. It was probably better that he go back to his empty house and be by himself.

"If I go, what should I bring?"

"What do you mean if? You just told Charlie you would. There was no if." She looked up, a bit of anger in her eyes, and confusion, like she couldn't imagine that he would say he was going to go and then not.

"All right. When I show up tomorrow, what should I bring?"

"Just yourself. That's what she said. After all, you're her guest. And Mom's too. Not mine."

"You texted her, so she came and asked."

Lark's cheeks pinked, and she smiled a little before she looked back down.

The look was so cute on her. He adored it. Adored her.

Of course, she could wear long johns and a gunnysack, and he would think she looked cute.

"So, if I were bringing something, what should I bring?"

"Just yourself," she repeated again, and that time, she looked up from her work, gave him a look that said she wasn't kidding, then looked back down. "We don't go real big on the gifts, there's ten of us, plus Mom. Plus like I said, we always have company. So, we usually get a couple of gifts for anyone who might show up, and everybody usually opens two. We don't go overboard, and it's not a big deal."

He supposed that made sense; when there were that many people in the family, gifts couldn't be the main reason people got together.

Well, his hamburger wasn't the greatest, but it was lean, and some people thought that was pretty good, so he'd take some of that as a housewarming gift or something. The way some people showed up with a wine bottle in their hands or whatever. And he would feel like he wasn't coming with nothing.

"Should I make something?"

She finished washing the cows, and they were both putting milkers on opposite ends of the milk house parlor, and she called back across to him, "Mom will have everything in hand, but if you want to make something, you're welcome to. You have all morning."

That was true, he would, but he had a couple of orders for birdhouses, and he was thinking about throwing another one of those together. He knew what he was going to spend his money on, and he wanted to make sure he had enough. He thought he was going to need more than what he had, and it was the one time that he was going to be able to do what he wanted to do, and no one would say anything. Therefore, he didn't want to go in without enough money in his pocket. To get what he wanted.

"All right," he said, figuring that if he brought something, it would be fine, and if he didn't, it would be fine as well. It didn't seem like the Stryker family was going to be picky.

The only thing he was picky about was getting to see Lark. He couldn't deny that there was a thrill that burst in his chest because he would see her on Christmas.

Chapter 18

"Look!" Lark said, standing beside the window in the milk parlor.

She didn't have to say anything else. Jeb came over immediately.

"Do you see? See the little beak sticking up? It's wide open. I bet if we were out there, we could hear it chirping."

"Do they chirp with their mouths open?"

"I don't know. But baby birds are loud. They must be able to, or else maybe it's just the brothers and sisters that are chirping while he's got his mouth open. Do you see it?" She looked over at Jeb, who stood beside her, his eyes facing the glass, squinting.

"Yeah. It's cute. How many are in there?"

"I'm not sure. There were four eggs, but I didn't check to see how many hatched. I didn't want to get too close."

"Are there babies in the other ones?"

"There's three eggs in one, and the last time I checked, there were five eggs in the one on the right. I was really excited for those, but then, I wasn't sure whether the parents will be able to take care of them."

She talked about what kind of bird they were and how it was unusual for them to leave five eggs at one time.

"I suppose we could go out to the manure pile and dig around a little bit. We could probably throw some worms on the ground to make it easy for them."

"Oh. I never thought of that. Bugs might be even better. I'll have to look up and see what they eat. I suppose we could scatter that around. Or...birdseed would probably work."

They looked back at the birdfeeder. It was full.

Lark had never filled it up herself, but she'd never seen it more than half-empty. Jeb made sure it stayed full all winter.

They had spent more than a few minutes while they were milking, standing at the window, waiting on cows to get done. After all, it was something a person couldn't hurry. While they waited, they enjoyed watching the birds that flew around.

"Looks to me like they might have everything they need, and there shouldn't be any reason why they can't raise five, unless one doesn't hatch."

"Yeah. I guess it's not too uncommon for them to lay more eggs than hatch. Or one just doesn't quite make it for some reason."

She was sad over the idea of a baby bird struggling and not living. It hurt her heart, even though she knew it was the natural thing. After all, God wanted the strongest to survive. To carry on.

The milkers started coming off, and they moved back into the parlor, working side by side.

"Are you still coming tonight?" Lark asked, as though Jeb had not told her he was thinking about it the last seventeen times she'd asked.

It was kind of like Christmas. She finally got him to go by getting her mom and her sister to ask him.

They were both okay with it, because she'd been careful about how she talked about him around the house. She'd made sure that everyone understood that he was a friend to her.

She could thank Clay for that. She probably had been a little bit too effusive, and for the most part, she'd managed to act like he was a friend and treat him like he was a friend.

The festival tonight was no different.

Except it was.

"I'm still thinking about it," Jeb said, but there was a grin lurking around his mouth. She didn't have any trouble recognizing that expression now.

"You've been planning on going all along, haven't you?" she accused as she dipped all the cows that were done, and they just had to wait on one.

"Maybe." He lifted his shoulder. "It's not like they haven't been planning this since last year this time."

It was true. The ladies of Sweet Water always started planning the next summer festival the day after the current one was over. She suspected sometimes they even started planning the next one before the current one was over.

But whatever it was, they had announced last summer that this year's festival would include an old-fashioned supper auction and dance, the day before they had a huge equipment auction.

In other words, the winning bidder would not only get supper when he bid on his lady, but he would also get a dance.

All the couples in Sweet Water were excited about it, and Lark, while she wasn't a part of a couple, had to say that she had a few dreams herself.

And of Jeb, of course.

Of course, she would have been happy regardless, since she graduated from high school, with honors, and while she had been accepted into all three colleges she applied for, two in North Dakota and one in Florida, she had every intention of staying right here.

She had turned eighteen with no fanfare two weeks prior.

She was pretty sure Jeb knew when her birthday was, because he'd offered her the morning off, but she declined.

Nothing else changed between them, and she had to admit she was a little disappointed. She kind of thought when she turned eighteen, he would have formally asked her to...be his girlfriend or something. She wasn't sure what, but maybe he was waiting for a special time.

Like tonight.

She could hardly contain her excitement. Hoping and praying that that was what it was.

She also had plans to keep her supper bucket back. She didn't want the bids to go too high on it so he couldn't afford it, so she was hoping that most people would have their buckets sold before hers, and all the big spenders would be happily eating with the girl of their choice.

That way, Jeb wouldn't have to spend too much on her.

Still, she didn't want to be too obvious. Maybe he had something else planned.

Of course, he pretended like he wasn't even going, but she suspected all along that he was planning to attend. They chatted the rest of the time, with Lark never quite getting up enough nerve to tell him what her bucket was going to look like.

It was all old-fashioned and quaint, but fun and exciting at the same time.

Married couples had the advantage of leaving the house together, although if her brothers were any indication, half the husbands wouldn't have a clue what their wives' buckets looked like when they arrived at the auction.

She could only imagine wives whispering to their husbands, "This one's mine."

She laughed at the thought, although she would be a little disappointed. It would say to her that her husband didn't care enough about her bucket to notice which one was hers.

Maybe husbands and wives got used to those kinds of things about each other, but she was really hoping she didn't have to tell Jeb to bid on hers. She hoped he would care enough to figure it out. Maybe spy on her when she was walking in, or maybe pay her sister to tell him which one was hers.

She laughed at both of those ideas.

"You seem a lot happier than you usually do, which is really saying something," Jeb said casually, leaning his shoulder against a support beam, crossing his arms over his chest as she put on the last milker.

"It's a happy day," she said with a jaunty smile.

She was still smiling half an hour later, and maybe she was whistling a little too, as they finished up, as she walked to her car and left.

She wasn't going to tell him which bucket was hers. She was sure he would figure it out himself.

Chapter 19

Jeb watched Lark drive away. It was the walk to and from the house where he really missed his dog. He supposed at night, he missed him following him in, lying down in his place in the corner of the kitchen. Missed looking over and seeing him there, and then, around eight o'clock or so, he would say, "Think it's about time we head to bed, don't you, Buster?"

They'd go to the stairs together, Buster following him, knowing it was time and exhausted after a long day of sleeping wherever Jeb was.

The idea made Jeb chuckle. It didn't matter where he went, Buster followed. And he acted like he had a big day, even though all he really did was sleep.

But no more. Jeb was almost used to it, but it really did make seeing Lark leave harder with no dog to keep him company.

He had no sooner made it in the house and thought about making himself a small sandwich to tide him over for the three or four hours it would be until he actually ate supper, hopefully food that Lark had made and put in her bucket, when he heard what sounded like a car crunching on the dry gravel outside.

It was a hot summer afternoon, and he had the windows open, so the sound was pretty noticeable.

Had Lark forgotten something?

Sometimes in the summer, she still rode there and back on her four-wheeler, even though she'd had a car for years. Even though she was now eighteen.

She was eighteen.

He tried not to think about that, because it meant, legally anyway, he could do whatever he wanted to do.

He was pretty sure she would be okay, even eager, to move forward with whatever that was.

Although he knew she had applied to and been accepted at three different colleges, she never said that she was actually going anywhere.

He didn't know whether it was too late to go or not. He supposed he should talk to her about it, but he was a bit of a coward and kept putting it off. He didn't want to make that final separation. Once he did that, once she left for college... He couldn't imagine not waking up every day looking forward to going out and seeing her smiling face. Couldn't imagine not walking her to her car, saying good night, then walking to his house with the warmth that lingered in his chest and heart after he'd seen her.

Couldn't imagine not having any of that.

By the time he walked across the kitchen to the door, the car had parked.

It was a large car, an expensive one, shiny, like it wasn't used to being driven off road.

He almost smiled at the thought, except the lady behind the wheel seemed to be struggling to get out.

He opened the door, took the steps two at a time, and walked to her car.

The woman looked up at him with eyes that were shrewd and interested. Like she had angles and was trying to figure out how to work him. It made him uncomfortable. She had ice-blue eyes, determined eyes, eyes that seemed to recognize him.

"Good evening, ma'am," he said as he opened the door.

She lifted her brows and looked impressed as she angled her head just so and said, "Why thank you, Jeb."

So she did know him.

Thanks to Lark, maybe just the way he knew she admired him and liked him exactly how he was, he had been able to loosen his tongue a bit more, and while he still didn't talk a lot, small talk such as good morning and good evening came easier.

But this woman knew his name, and it threw him.

He stood with the door open, his hand on the latch, staring at her.

"Are you going to help a tired lady out?"

He narrowed his eyes. Did he recognize her?

"I see you don't recognize me." She put her hand out until he took it, and leaned heavily on their joined appendages as she got out of the car. "Sorry, I'm in the middle of my cancer treatments, and they're taking a toll on me."

"I see."

"I'm Donna Omon. I was friends with your parents back in the day. I'm a bit younger than they were, but we were friends at one time."

"I vaguely remember you. You and your husband had a farm a couple of hours away. The area where my mom came from."

"That's right. She and her family and my family were friends, and we stayed that way for a while, although we drifted apart in her later years. I was raising children, and her girls were older. Then you came along, and mine were older. It's sad sometimes to think how life slips by." The lady sounded a little upset and melancholy, but he supposed if he had cancer, he'd be thinking pretty hard about his life, too.

"Mind if I sit on your porch for a little bit? I have something I want to talk to you about."

"You're welcome on my porch anytime. A friend of my mother's is a friend of mine."

He thanked Lark in his head for giving him more confidence. The words came a lot easier, and he wanted to think it was interesting what the love of a good woman could do, but he couldn't let his mind go there. Lark's love wasn't his.

Lark wasn't his.

When she had chosen a seat on the porch, he offered her water. It was all he had, but she declined.

He was tempted to go in and get a drink for himself, but he didn't want to have one while she didn't, so he waited for her to settle on the swing, and then he leaned against the banister, his arms crossed over his chest, one foot crossed over the other, casual, waiting.

"All right, I'm sure you're thinking I might be here to reminisce or something of the sort," she said.

He had no idea why she might be there, but he supposed reminiscing was as good of a reason as any. He didn't mind hearing about his parents or his sisters, since they were so much older than he was. Sometimes the stories he heard about them felt like they came from another family.

But the lady didn't say anything about them, she just continued on. "So I'll just get straight to the point."

"All right." He liked people like that. People who didn't waste words, didn't give him a bunch of platitudes before they said what they really wanted.

"I'm dying."

Whoa. That was unexpected.

He wasn't quite sure what to say. With Lark, he could talk about death, he could say what was on his heart, because he felt safe with her. Comfortable. Like she knew him well enough to understand if he said something wrong, she wouldn't hold it against him or think he was weird.

"My kids want to send me to a nursing home. They've already sold my house."

"I'm sorry."

"That's fine. It's not your fault. They're trying to declare me mentally incapable. So far, they haven't been successful."

"Good." He wasn't sure what else to say but figured she was pausing for him to put words in. Seemed to be what people did. Just make sure he hadn't fallen asleep or something.

"But I am in full control of my faculties as you can plainly see."

"It's pretty obvious to me, ma'am."

"Call me Donna."

"All right, Miss Donna."

"Just Donna."

"Donna."

He wasn't sure why that was so important to her, but he could do what she asked. Or at least try.

She looked satisfied when she heard her name on his lips. She continued. "Anyway, as I am in full control of my brain, and I happen to still enjoy using it, I came up with a plan to foil my children."

That made him uncomfortable. He didn't want to make anyone mad. Particularly this lady's children, since he didn't really know any of them.

But he didn't say anything, and she continued without him.

"You are a key player in my plan."

"All right."

"Farming has never been a profitable venture. You're land rich but cash poor. My house got sold, but it was still in my name, and so now I am land poor but cash rich. It happened to be on a rather large and well-known oil field, and the amount of money that I got for my land is quite a lot. We're talking tens of millions of dollars."

He whistled low. His farm wasn't on any oil fields, although even if it were, he wouldn't want to sell. He loved it. Loved sitting on the front porch, looking at the view he'd looked at all his life. From the time he could remember, he sat on this porch and looked out over the horizon, thinking about what was over there, watching the sun go down, looking forward to the day ahead, and doing it all again. He loved it.

"I don't want to be put in a home. I don't want to be shoved aside, I don't want to be pushed away like some kind of old piece of garbage." The woman's voice seemed a little angry, and he couldn't blame her. If that's what her children were trying to do, she had every right to be angry about it. He would be.

"I want to live the rest of my life, no matter whether I live six months or several more years, I want to live it the way I want to. And I've figured out a way to make that happen."

He wasn't going to fight her kids for her if that was what she was thinking.

"I decided the best way to do that would be to get married."

All right, so did she want him to find her a husband? Talk someone into marrying her? Allow them to get married on his farm?

He had no idea where she was going with this conversation, so he just waited.

"I had my lawyer draw up a prenup. I can't do this with my kids, but I can do it with my husband." She cackled a little.

It made him uncomfortable, but he covered it well, he thought. He had a pretty good poker face.

"The prenup says that my husband will not at any time send me to a nursing home. That I will live at his house for the rest of my life, and he will take care of me. If he has to hire someone to help him, that's fine. My money is his to spend as he wishes, as long as he does that one thing for the rest of my life."

The woman had been confident in her speech, but at that last part, when she talked about her death, her eyes dropped.

"It's probably not going to be long. The cancer isn't responding to chemo, and there aren't a whole lot of options left. I want to die with dignity, my way." She lifted her eyes. "I visited your mother on this farm multiple times before when her girls were young. When you were little. I loved it. It's beautiful. She made the house a home, and there was always peace and joy here. I have a lot of good memories sitting on this porch, shelling peas, laughing about things that young ladies laugh about, and watching the sun go down."

He had memories there too, and he couldn't fault her, but he just nodded.

He still wasn't sure how that had anything to do with him, so he looked out over the horizon and hoped she got to the point soon. He didn't want to be late to the festival tonight. Didn't want to be late, because he needed to see what Lark's bucket looked like so he could bid on the right one.

He'd been looking forward to this for so long, saving, building birdhouses so he could afford to bid no matter how high her bucket went, and with brothers, he figured it would be high, but he didn't want to miss tonight.

"I want you to marry me. I want you to sign the prenup, and the millions of dollars that I have will be yours."

Jeb froze, then his eyes flew to hers.

Milk prices had dropped. He was holding onto the farm by his fingernails. He'd wanted for a long time to increase Lark's wage which was ridiculously low. But he couldn't. He couldn't afford it. If she quit, he would be working by himself, because it was all he could do to pay the mortgage and the feed bill.

If he married this woman, he would have millions of dollars to pay off the farm. To make improvements. To...do whatever the farm needed.

"When I die, it all goes to you. That's in the prenup too. And just in case you think that I'm going to marry you, then spend all of my money, I don't want anything, other than my freedom." The woman gave a sniff. "And if it worries you that bad, I can have the lawyer put in that you get half the money up front. I'd keep half, just in case you don't keep your word. I want to have the means to hire lawyers to fight you."

She was a confident woman. Determined. And a little bit sour.

Not appealing at all, not even in a grandmotherly type of way, but for millions of dollars... And for just a short while.

Jeb could do it.

He could marry her, inherit her money, and when Lark was done with vet school, he would have something to offer her. Something worthwhile. Something more than a lifetime of drudgery, working from before the sun came up until after it went down day in and day out, constant hard work, with no break or end in sight. A life that would be even harder if they had children, and...the idea of Lark having his children was something he had never allowed himself to entertain, but if he did this, they could afford it.

His children with Lark.

He kept his arms folded over his chest, kept his face impassive, and stared at the screen door, where the orange glow of the sunset turned the small wires of the screen a golden yellow, making it seem to shimmer in the evening air.

He needed to get ready. He needed to go. Lark would be expecting him.

"How long do I have?" he asked.

The woman coughed for a good while, the congestion in her chest making it sound like she was going to cough up a lung before she was finished.

Finally, she was done, and she said, "I can give you a couple of days, but I want to get this taken care of. My children have lawyers on the case, and they're determined to have me declared incompetent. My lawyer is fighting it, of course, but the sooner we get married and get this implemented, the better."

She lifted her chin. She was a proud lady, but he could look into her eyes and see that he was her last hope.

"Please," she said softly.

He didn't feel the same pull with her that he did with Lark. Lark didn't have to say please. She didn't have to beg, and she didn't have to ask twice. If he could do it for her, he was on it.

But there was a part of him that, aside from the money, always wanted to help.

This lady was no different. Of course, marrying her without the money wouldn't do anybody any good, but since Lark was unavailable and would be for another seven years, he could totally do this. This woman didn't look like she was going to last another month, let alone a year or seven.

But he didn't want to make a rash decision, and he really didn't want to make the decision tonight. He'd been looking forward to tonight, just eating with Lark, dancing with her, for...a year. Ever since he'd heard of it, he'd known that she would be eighteen, known that he might not be able to do anything in private, because he wouldn't want to start something that would be too hard to stop. But with the whole town watching, he was pretty sure he could hold her in his arms and dance a respectful dance with her.

Even if he wasn't a dancer, even if he hated to have eyes on him, even if the crowds weren't his thing, even if this was not something that he would normally do, he would do it for Lark.

He'd been looking forward to it.

"I'll give you an answer tomorrow."

He didn't move, other than to turn his head to look at her.

His arms were still crossed, and so were his legs, his stance casual, but his heart thundered hard.

It was thundering because he knew his answer was going to be yes.

Chapter 20

Lark hummed and twirled and tried hard not to float into the community center.

She looked around and had not seen Jeb's old farm pickup, but she didn't allow that to put a damper on her mood at all.

Normally, everywhere she went she wore jeans and a T-shirt, but she had spent some of the money that she had saved, just a little of it, at the secondhand store in Rockerton, and bought herself a dress that floated around her like a cloud.

She'd never had a dress like this before, a light, airy, bright white dress that hugged her torso and draped in billowing whispers down her legs, tied to her waist with a dark blue sash.

The scooped neckline wasn't low enough to show her farmer's tan, and the flutter sleeves hid the fact that her arms were white from her shoulder to four inches down above her elbow.

It didn't matter, the dress made her feel like a princess.

Her mom had done her hair, combing it until it sparkled and curling it so that it fell in luscious waves around her shoulders.

For the first time in her life, she felt beautiful.

And she was eighteen, the man she loved was coming tonight, and she didn't know how he was going to do it, but he was going to bid on her bucket, he was going to win it, and he was going to dance with her.

After he did that, she was going to tell him that she loved him and ask him to marry her.

She couldn't wait.

Looking back, Lark figured there were times in a person's life when things went exactly the way they were supposed to, exactly the way a person had envisioned them, exactly the way a person had dreamed and planned and hoped.

Those times were few and far between, but they did happen.

Of course, most often, they didn't. Most often, a person had dreams, and they never turned out quite the way they wanted them to.

She supposed God couldn't give her everything she wanted, because then she would grow up spoiled, just like children who got whatever they wanted.

For most of her life, that was how it had happened for Lark. She hadn't quite gotten what she wanted. Nothing ever turned out exactly the way she dreamed.

But that night, the night of the auction and dance, was the stuff of dreams.

She had set her box back, so it was late when the auctioneer finally picked it and held it up. There were only three other ladies waiting to have their buckets auctioned off, and they were all married.

There was no doubt that the box was hers, so even if Jeb was late, as she suspected he was, he would know exactly whose box it was.

And he did. He bid on it. Her brothers gave him a hard time, and he ended up paying one hundred and twenty-seven dollars for his meal. She didn't ask where he got the money, although she worried about it a little. She'd read about milk prices, knew they'd gone down, and at times, they'd even talked about the farm and finances. He hadn't seemed like he really wanted to hold anything back from her, and any question she asked, he answered.

But she hadn't asked for a while, because she didn't want to be depressed. Didn't want to see his worry and struggle. Just wanted to do everything she could to make life easier for him. Still, the idea that the farm was slowly sinking down was never far from her thoughts. But it didn't matter. As long as they were together, they would figure something out. What they figured out, she wasn't sure, but they would figure out something.

Still, he bid on her box, beat her brothers, to much laughter and teasing, and had gone up to claim his box while she went up to meet him.

"I'm sorry about my brothers," she said after he'd taken the box and accepted the congratulations from the auctioneer, amid the clapping of all of the other people who had stopped to watch until the show had died down.

"They're just being brothers," he said, smiling down at her, like he didn't have a care in the world and she was the most amazing thing he'd ever seen, like he admired her and thought she was pretty. "You're beautiful. I've never seen anything as beautiful as you. That includes every sunset I've ever seen, every sunrise. Every newborn calf, every cow that makes it through surgery, every pure white drop of milk that comes out of the tank."

They weren't the pretty poetry words that someone else might spout, but she knew how much those things meant to him. How beautiful the milk was, how special it was when a cow that they thought might not make it got up and walked into the parlor by herself.

She understood the beauty in all of those things and saw his words for the compliment that they were.

They made her heart glow, her eyes sparkle, and they put even more of a spring in her step than had been there before.

Not only did she feel beautiful, but she knew the man she loved thought she was beautiful. And that's all she ever wanted.

Chapter 21

"All right, fellows, grab your partner for the dance she owes you."

Jeb stopped. He'd just paid for his winning bid—he'd had more than enough money to cover it from the birdhouses he'd sold—and had been about to grab Lark's hand.

"May I have this dance?" he asked, low and slow, and hoping she would say yes.

She was the most beautiful thing he'd ever seen. Her eyes glowed, her cheeks were red, her hair flowing in soft waves around her shoulders, hair he hardly ever saw since she always wore it up on the farm.

She wore some kind of soft, flirty dress that shimmered and moved as she did, although she could be wearing a feed sack, and he'd still think she was the most beautiful thing he'd ever seen. It almost made his eyes hurt to look at her, and it definitely made his heart sore.

When she smiled and nodded, uncharacteristically quiet, he couldn't help but smile back, both sides of his mouth lifting up and a few teeth showing as well. A huge smile for him, but he couldn't help himself.

Maybe he was seeing her through new eyes, eyes that knew that tomorrow he would have to go home and make the hard decision, but tonight...tonight he got to spend with the girl he'd been in love with for the last three years.

He reached a hand down and slid his fingers down her wrist, twining her fingers with his, until their hands joined them together. Her skin was soft, smooth, and perfect. He wanted to do more than just touch her hands, he wanted to run his fingers over her neck, down her shoulder, touch her cheeks and her nose, her eyes and her lips. Everywhere.

His hand tingled with the desire. But he swallowed and said, "Let me put this aside," indicating her lunch box.

She nodded, and he walked to the nearest piece of furniture, which happened to be a chair, and he set the box down.

He didn't want to waste a second of their dancing time, especially because he knew that this was his last chance. His only chance.

If, and that was a huge if, she was still single when she graduated from vet school, he'd be at her doorstep, begging her to take him, but the promise that he made to Clay rang in his ears, and he knew even tonight he had to watch his step.

He could hold her hand, dance with her, because he bought that right, but...after tonight ended, he had to let her go.

The floor was crowded as the first strands of music played, but since they were some of the last to purchase their meals, they were still up at the end, so he was able to find a corner that was not private but less crowded.

He pulled her to him, not wanting to hold onto her hand when he could hold onto the actual woman.

"Is this okay?" he asked softly as he put one arm around her waist and the other around her shoulders.

It was the closest they'd ever been, but she wrapped her arms around his waist easily and nodded her head, her forehead brushing his cheek, him breathing her scent. It was pure and sweet and fresh, and it smelled absolutely perfect. Like home, like family, like a comfortable chair in front of a warm fire. Sweet and perfect.

Her body, supple and strong, warmed his hands and pressed against him, feeling soft and good.

His lungs sputtered, but his soul sighed in satisfaction, like they were standing on his porch watching the sunset after a hard day's work and everything was right with the world.

Music started to play, and a woman sang about having a dance for the rest of her life, and Jeb had to stop listening. He didn't get a dance for the rest of his life. He got this one dance. That was it.

He closed his eyes and rested his cheek against her temple, swaying slowly to the music without really caring about the beat, just feeling the graceful movements of the woman under his hands and wishing this moment could last forever.

They didn't talk at all during the dance. He barely opened his eyes. Thankfully, they didn't run into anyone. That would have ruined the moment, but he worked with all his heart and soul to memorize every second, every heartbeat, every breath she took, every slide of her body under his fingers, every touch of her skin.

The music stopped. Something fast with a driving beat came on, totally ill-suited for his contemplative and romantic mood, and he reluctantly pulled away from her, sliding his fingers down her arm and clasping their hands together again.

Her expression was a little dreamy as well, and he could only hope that she enjoyed that as much as he did.

Of course, it wasn't enough. It wasn't nearly enough.

"Are you ready to eat?" He wasn't the slightest bit hungry. Whoever said they could live on love, it was the absolute truth. He didn't want to eat, didn't want to sleep, didn't want to do anything but pull her back into his arms and never let her go.

Maybe he shouldn't have tried to do this tonight. Maybe he should have just stayed home. He would know exactly what he was missing now. For almost a decade, he wouldn't forget this, because it was all he had.

"Let's go outside," she said softly, looking up into his eyes with anticipation in her own.

He wasn't sure what the anticipation was for, unless she was just looking forward to eating with him as much as he was looking forward to eating with her.

As he walked to the chair where her meal bucket was, holding Lark's hand with his own, relishing how it felt to have her beside him, so close he could feel the heat of her body, feel the brush of her hips against him as her dress wrapped around his legs with each stride, he happened to look up and meet the eyes of Clay Stryker.

Clay did not look angry. He didn't look like he was about ready to come over and say anything.

He just looked.

That was all Jeb needed to remind him that he had made promises, and he needed to keep them.

He didn't know what his own face said, although his position beside Lark, close enough that their sides brushed when they walked, her hand held in his, not dangling between them, but he carried it pressed to his chest, didn't look at all like he was going to be a man who kept his word, but hopefully Clay could see from his expression that he had only Lark's best interest at heart.

Surely Clay understood he could have one night with her. Not even a night, a few precious hours, before he lost her…forever maybe. It was possible. But at least for eight long years.

He gave an almost imperceptible nod of his head. Clay's eyes narrowed for just a moment before his head nodded in return, a thoughtful expression on his face, but no worries, just confidence that Jeb would keep his word.

Jeb appreciated that vote of confidence, and he determined in his heart yet again that he would do the best thing for Lark, no matter what it cost him.

He pushed the outside door open with the hand that held the box of food, not wanting to let go of Lark's hand for even a second.

"Where?" he asked, leaving it up to her.

"Do you mind going to the graveyard?" she asked softly, nodding with her head toward the old white church and the graveyard behind it. It was deserted, although couples mingled around the parking lot, couples like them who wanted a little more privacy than the bustling community center offered.

He didn't answer, just started walking toward it. He didn't mind graveyards at all. One day, he'd be in one. That's where he'd end up until the rapture, so he might as well get used to them.

They were a good reminder, like he told Lark so long ago when he lost Buster. He wasn't afraid of dying. It inspired him to do better. To do his very best, because a person never knew when the cold fingers of death were going to wrap around their heart, take them away.

It made him live with purpose, live with determination to do his very best every day.

"I've never forgotten what you said about dying," Lark said softly.

She wanted to talk about dying today? He wanted to talk about living. Living and loving and life. But only life tonight. Not tomorrow when everything would change.

"I can't imagine I ever had anything inspiring to say," he murmured. If he got any words out, ever, they were most definitely not inspiring, and that was the truth. His words never sounded good once they left his head.

"You're the most inspiring person I know," Lark said. Her words were light, and she gave him a small smile as she leaned into his side a little, allowing him to hold her hand close to his chest, allowing their thighs to brush, her skirt to wrap around his legs, her scent to mingle with his. Her warmth beside him.

A warm breeze brushed their skin, ruffling her dress as he opened the squeaky gate to the graveyard, and she stepped lightly in.

He didn't let go of her hand, and she had to wait while he turned around and balanced the box while closing the gate.

They were the only ones who'd decided to go into the cemetery, the only ones who apparently found death romantic, or a reminder of the preciousness of life, maybe, so they were completely alone, although the sounds of conversation reached them over the night air, and occasionally shadowy figures went by in the distance. The light blinked out for a second as figures walked in front of it, and the door to the community center opened and closed.

They were close to everyone else but not so close that they couldn't have a private conversation.

"I should be starving, because I haven't eaten since lunch, but I'm not the slightest bit hungry." Lark smiled as they sat down on the bench underneath the big drooping oak tree.

He set the box down, and then he settled down beside Lark, his arm over the back of the bench.

He wasn't expecting it, but she wiggled just a little, coming closer to him and curling up in the crook of his arm. Their sides pressed together, her head leaning on his shoulder.

He wanted to bring his arm off the back of the bench and curl it around her, pulling her even closer, but instead, his fingers gripped the old wood, and he kept his arm right where it was.

They were quiet for just a bit, and the aroma of fried chicken wafted up. He wasn't hungry, but he almost asked if they could eat, just because he didn't want her to have wasted her time and not have someone appreciate her efforts.

They were going to need to go their separate ways, but he didn't want her to think that there was ever anything she had done for him that he didn't appreciate.

On that idea, he opened his mouth. "You worked for me for a long time, and I have barely paid you anything. I... I didn't want you to think that I thought that was all you were worth."

"I've seen the news. I know what milk prices are. I also know that last week, when I asked if you were making hay, and you said no, it wasn't because you didn't want to."

He took in a breath but didn't say anything.

"The tractor's been broken all winter, and motor repairs are expensive."

That was exactly right. He had been saving, a little bit at a time, because he couldn't stand to take his tractor to be repaired knowing he didn't have the money to pay for the repairs. He couldn't expect someone else to make a living doing repair work for him for free. He was a business owner too. He knew that people couldn't do work without getting paid for it. Especially work that took parts, like motor repair.

"I'll have enough next week," he finally said.

"There's an auction tomorrow. I was walking through all of the things that are offered for sale, and there's a lot of farm equipment. Several tractors that look like they're in good repair, and while they're not quite as big as the one you have, they'll run the baler and pull the wagon."

Chapter 22

Jeb had considered buying a used tractor. It would almost, not quite, but almost, be cheaper to buy a used tractor than it would be to get his old one repaired.

"It costs about the same to repair my old one as it does to buy a used one."

"You might get a deal at the auction."

"True."

He had no plans to go to the auction. Tomorrow, if things went the way they were looking, he would probably be driving to Rockerton to get married to Donna.

It was the first time in a long time that he was going to do something and he wasn't going to talk to Lark about it first. He didn't want to spoil tonight by talking about tomorrow.

He also didn't want to spoil tonight by talking about the money he didn't have. Although, it wasn't because he hadn't worked for it, it wasn't even because he had made poor decisions. His dad was the one who had borrowed the money for the parlor. When Jeb had taken over the farm, he had to borrow money to pay off his sisters' shares, and then he'd taken over the payments on the mortgage.

"Jeb?"

"Yeah?" he asked, moving his head just slightly so his cheek brushed over her hair, and he breathed her scent in, deep and pure. He could stay like this forever.

"I turned eighteen two weeks ago."

"I know. I have a birthday present for you, but..."

"But what?" she asked, and there was a note of excitement he wasn't expecting.

"But I thought maybe it wasn't appropriate for me to give it to you."

"Appropriate? Why wouldn't it be? I'm an adult. I'm eighteen, I graduated from high school, and we can—"

"You have college."

"I don't want to go to college. I want to—"

"You have vet school."

"I don't want to be a vet anymore. I just want to be—"

"You're going to college, to vet school, and you're not thinking about anything else until those things are done."

Those were words he wanted to say, truly. He wanted the best for her, and he knew that was what her heart's desire had always been. He couldn't see her throwing it all away for him. But he probably wouldn't have said them if it hadn't been for his promise to Clay. After all, she was in his arms tonight, wanting to stay. Almost begging to stay. She didn't have to beg, she didn't even have to ask, all she had to do was indicate that she might want to, and he would do everything in his power to see that she did.

Whatever it took.

But he couldn't break his promise.

"Jeb. I know what I want. And that's not it."

"You love animals. You're brilliant. And you can help them by being a vet. I know you can. But it just takes time."

"I don't want to waste that much time of my life in school. I want to spend it with you."

"You just said it. There's nothing on the farm. Nothing but back-breaking hard work, bills that need to be paid and not enough money to pay them, stuff that breaks down, and a hard life that will wear you out." He took a breath. He wasn't good at this. He'd compared her to cows earlier. "You're beautiful. You have so much life, so much energy. So much beauty in your heart and soul. You have character and integrity, compassion and kindness. You bring joy and sunshine wherever you go. I love your heart, your soul, the way you see people and love them. The way you saw me."

She had seen him in a way no one else ever had. Maybe just because she'd taken the time to look. Hadn't just seen what everyone else had but had looked beyond the words he couldn't say and had loved him despite his flaws and faults.

"You can't let that all die on the farm as you give your heart and soul, and it sucks all of the life out of you. Not having money, not knowing whether you're going to be able to pay the bills, whether the bank is going to take the farm, not being able to make the hay you know your cows need because you can't afford to fix the tractor, those things will kill you."

She shook her head, fast, like she couldn't wait for him to be done talking before she started. "Sitting on the front porch, watching the sunset, watching our children play in the yard, knowing that we're together, whether it's on the farm, or whether it's somewhere else, it doesn't matter. Just having you beside me, that's all I want. I can do anything, we can do anything, as long as we're together." She lifted her face up to his. "Don't you see that? What we have is so unusual. People don't get this. It doesn't come to everyone, not even once in a lifetime, it's more rare than that. You and I have it. Our hearts talk. Our hearts see each other."

She moved so that her body was tilted toward him, and her hand lifted to his cheek.

"I love the farm, love the animals, and love the house and everything in it, but it's you. You are what matters to me."

He closed his eyes, put his hand over hers, and pressed the warmth against his cheek. Then, he turned his head slowly and kissed the palm of her hand. "I don't deserve to have you say those words to me. I don't deserve to have you feel any of those things for me. And you can't. You have other things you need to do. You can't waste everything that God has given you on me."

"It's not wasted."

Her hand slipped down, and it rested on his chest where the box that he had for her sat in his pocket.

He would have given it to her on her birthday, but he was a little embarrassed. He hadn't been sure the money he had saved selling birdhouses would be enough to buy her box at the auction tonight, so he'd just bought her something small for her birthday.

He knew Lark was used to not having much, but he wanted her to have everything.

Which was another reason he had to let her go. She wasn't going to have everything if she was rotting on the farm for the rest of her life.

"You have your hand on your birthday present," he said.

She smiled. "Does this mean I can open it?"

He nodded.

Her eyes glowed, and she pulled the box out of his pocket, holding it up.

It was too big to be a ring box, but it was pretty obvious it was a piece of jewelry.

"I can't believe you got me something." She laughed a little. "I was kind of disappointed when I thought you forgot it. It...hurt my heart a little, even though I didn't care if you got me anything, it was just the idea that you didn't think about me."

How could she think that? He never stopped thinking about her.

"I thought about you, Lark. I always think about you. I just... I can't always act on those thoughts."

Boy, that was the truth.

She glowed up at him, and he was so tempted to lower his head, but he didn't.

"Open it," he urged, now that she had it out.

The smile on her face went straight to his heart as she moved the box one direction then another before her head lowered, and her fingers slid the paper off, and she opened the small jewelry box.

The gold links sparkled in the starlight, and Lark held it so that it reflected the glow from the community building.

"It's so beautiful and delicate. A necklace, a bird," she breathed, and her look showed that she loved that he'd gotten something he knew she loved.

"A lark."

She laughed a little, and then one finger came up while she touched it carefully. "So beautiful."

"It's you."

He didn't think of her as a bird exactly, but he knew she loved them, and her name was fitting. He'd seen the necklace and knew it was perfect for her. Knew he wanted to give her something that she would carry close to her, against her chest. Since that's where his heart lived.

She carefully took it out of its little box and held it up. "Would you put it on me?"

He didn't know if his big, clumsy fingers could work the delicate clasp, but Lark did not have to ask twice. He'd do anything for her, and he took it from her hand, unhooking it carefully, as the delicate chain shimmered in the dim light, and Lark turned her back to him, pulling her hair to one side and lifting it up.

He put the necklace over her head and then pulled both ends around behind her neck, slender and graceful, and as delicate as the chain that lay against it.

He probably shouldn't have done it, but he leaned forward and pressed his lips to the slender column of her neck, just below her hairline.

She sighed, soft on the night air, like she wanted him to do it again. But he closed his eyes instead, breathed deeply of the air that had been warmed by her skin, before he shifted back and finished fastening the necklace.

"You are far more beautiful than any necklace, but you make it look beautiful," he said as she turned toward him, the lark nestled against her chest.

"You make me feel beautiful," she said softly, her words sincere and a little dreamy as she met his eyes.

The night, the stars, the gentle rustling of the breeze, the soft laughter of other couples on the air, the silent privacy of the grave-yard, and the reminder to make every day count swirled around him. It felt heady and it jumbled his thoughts, spinning them in his head until he couldn't grab hold of them, wasn't sure whether the night was a dream, or whether it was real, with the soft, warm body of Lark pressed against his, and her eyes shining up at him, and those moments being the culmination of years of dreaming and wondering what it would be like, what it would feel like, what he would do if they were ever this close.

Maybe he was a little befuddled, maybe he was just so deeply in the moment he couldn't think, but when her body shifted just a little, and her head lifted up, and her lips found his, it was shocking and surprising and unexpected, and yet felt so right and so real and so completely perfect and exactly what he always wanted that he didn't even think about pulling away.

Instead, he pressed closer, his arms going around her, pulling her toward him, pressing her tight against his chest, while her hands buried in his hair, wrapping around his neck, moving down his back until he wasn't sure where he stopped and she started because they were so close and it felt so perfect.

Long moments passed when all of his senses were surrounded by everything that was Lark, her touch, her soft sighs, her taste and her scent, and the warmth he felt, strong and graceful, soft and perfect under her dress.

It was him that moved back first. He was pretty sure that Lark would be content to kiss him all night long, and he would have been more than content to let her, but...he shouldn't have kissed her to begin with.

Still, he didn't want to let her go, didn't want to ruin the moment, and he moved his lips over her cheek, across her temple, and buried them in the hair above her ear while he whispered, "That was better than a million dreams, and this has been the best night of my life."

"We'll have a thousand more nights like this, tens of thousands, marry me."

Lark's whispered words felt warm and wonderful in his head and brain and heart, and he wanted to say, *of course. As soon as possible.*

He didn't. He couldn't. But he couldn't tell her no either. Couldn't shatter the beauty of the evening. Wanted this memory to be the best memory he had, and hopefully it would be a good one for her too.

"Let's not talk about that tonight," he said instead, moving his hands down her back, brushing his lips against her temple, then slowly moving back. He didn't want to, wanted to hold her forever, but there needed to be space between them. They couldn't sit here on the bench and kiss all night. As nice as that would be.

Her companionship, her chatter, her laughter and conversation had always been the best things about her, and he wanted those memories too.

"Let's eat," he said, even though he wasn't the slightest bit hungry. Felt like he wouldn't be able to eat for years. Whether it was because of the knowledge that he was losing everything he loved, or whether it was just true that love filled a man to the very top, and he didn't need anything else. "I hate to see all the work you put into the food go to waste," he added when he caught her sigh of disappointment.

He could echo that. Could sigh the exact same way. But his words made her smile, and she moved, reluctantly, away, reaching over and grabbing the box.

They ate together, laughed together, talked about everything and nothing, things that weren't important, things that they loved, and at times they sat in silence, the meal all gone, the parking lot emptying out, and the air becoming heavy and ripe with the knowledge that they needed to part.

"Can I take you home?" The words came from somewhere out of his brain, even though he didn't want to say them, because they signaled the end of the best night of his life.

"You can, but I drove. And I don't know how I'd get my car back."

He wanted to take her home, wanted to kiss her good night at her doorstep, wanted there to be just one time where they had what could be called a date, even if he didn't pick her up.

But he supposed he'd gotten far more tonight than he ever thought he would have, and as a beggar, he shouldn't be greedy.

They'd already agreed that since she was helping with the festival, helping her mom, her brothers, and working wherever the Sweet Water ladies needed her, that he would milk by himself in the morning.

He supposed at some point, he was going to need to do something to let her know that they weren't going to be together again, although maybe if he got married, the rumors would reach her, and she wouldn't have memories of a big blowup with him.

No. He'd tell her. Tomorrow. He'd find a way to tell her tomorrow, when the magic of tonight wouldn't be ruined.

He helped her gather the things up and held her hand close to his chest again as they walked through the gate and toward her car which was parked at the side of the lot.

It was the only car left in that section, and he didn't really plan it, but after they'd set the box in the back seat and he stood with his hand on her door latch and he opened her door for her, she stepped into his arms, and he lowered his head again, as natural as breathing, and kissed her, soft and sweet, until his desperation and longing and years of wanting her took over, and the kiss turn into something wild and far more passionate than he had intended.

When he lifted his head, Lark was pressed against the back door of her car, his body tight against hers and her arms holding him as tight as she could.

She made a sound of protest when he lifted his head, and he pressed his cheek against her temple while the words he didn't want to say spilled out.

"I love you."

He shouldn't have said it. Shouldn't have let the words out, but it was the only thing beating around in his brain, tramping through his conscience, whirling and swirling and entangling with the rational thoughts, the ones that knew what he had to do in the morning versus the ones that he wanted to do tonight.

Two different women, completely different feelings, and a sacrifice so big it felt impossible.

"I love you, too. I always have." Lark kissed his chin, her lips soft and warm and so close he could hardly resist the temptation to turn his head and touch them with his again. "Marry me. Please."

"College. Vet school."

Clay would never know what those words and his promise cost him.

"I don't have the money for any of that anyway, even if I did want to go, which I don't."

"You have the money." Before he paid any bills on the farm, before he did anything else, the first thing he was going to do was to make sure that Lark could afford every single year of schooling, every piece of equipment she needed, every book, every paper, every bite of food, from now until she graduated with her doctorate of veterinary medicine degree.

He would do that, make sure of that, if it was the last thing he did.

"I don't want the money. I want you." Lark's words were soft, maybe a little tortured, but full of the hopes and dreams and innocence of youth.

"And I want you. Sometimes we don't get what we want." He ran his lips over her incredibly soft skin and whispered, his words coming out rough, "And sometimes we have to wait."

He took a deep breath and stepped back, putting his hand on the door and meeting her eyes with his.

She looked a little confused, a lot sad, and very bereft. But her lips pressed together, knowing this wasn't the time to argue, before she said, "Thank you for tonight. It was magical. The best night of my life by far."

"Same. So much the same."

She stepped forward quickly, pressing her lips once more to his, before she said, "You'll be hearing from me tomorrow." She gave him a little smile, a saucy wave, looking so much like the Lark he knew and loved, before she settled down in her car, tucking her gauzy skirt around her legs before he closed the door behind her.

Maybe she'd hear from him first. He needed to tell her face-to-face, but that was for tomorrow. It would ruin tonight.

With that thought, he stepped back as she started her car, and he watched as she pulled slowly out of the lot, waving to him, blowing him a kiss.

He stood with what he knew had to be a sappy grin on his face as he watched her leave. Taking his heart with her.

He would do what needed to be done tomorrow, would do what he had promised Clay years ago. He would keep his word. He would do the very best thing for Lark, would provide the way for her to do what God created her to do, would do his best to see her start on her way to becoming a vet.

She would be angry with him, but Lark didn't hold grudges. There might be a future for them, but not for at least eight years. Those eight years felt like a lifetime.

Chapter 23

Jeb walked slowly to the house from the barn the next morning. The milking was done, later than usual since he had done it himself.

It was the first time in a really long time that Lark hadn't been at the barn with him in the morning, and it had been lonely and quiet. He'd not just gotten used to her happy chatter, her crazy comments, and the way she spent the first thirty-five minutes of every morning trying to make him laugh, but he found himself craving it, addicted to...to Lark.

He'd looked at the birds by himself, seen the mama bird with her babies, the mom going into the nest with the babies in the birdhouse he'd made for Lark. Saw birds of every kind flying around the feeder.

Looked around at the parlor and the cows and everything just seemed dark and empty without Lark.

But he needed to get used to it. Today was the first day of the rest of his life, and there were going to be a lot of years, long and hard, without her, while she went and did what she was born to do.

He had kept his promise. He would let her go.

He cooked himself a couple of eggs, made some toast, and thought about Buster. Wished he was still with him.

He supposed he should go look for another pup but just couldn't get the gumption up right away. Didn't really feel like doing any-thing.

He probably should talk to Donna about it. He didn't know how long she had left, but it would be rude of him to get a dog if she were allergic or didn't want one.

He checked the calendar, noted that the milk check should arrive in ten days, and did a few quick calculations to make sure he was going to have enough money to pay for the tractor repairs.

None too soon either. He should have been making hay two weeks ago, but with the milk price being down, he'd sold a couple of cows, and he could get through the winter with less this year.

That seemed to be what farming was, getting through with less.

Less, a lot less without Lark. He felt like he lost the sun and all the warmth and light it gave and entered the dark night of a years-long winter.

Around eleven o'clock, the fancy, expensive car pulled up, and he stepped out on the porch as Donna got out.

She looked a little different this morning, slightly younger, maybe the sun was kinder to her, or maybe his eyes were just cloudy with the tears he'd never cry.

He walked down the stairs and opened the door for her.

He might not want to marry her, definitely didn't love her, but manners were manners, and courtesy was courtesy.

He wasn't going to be unkind to her, just because she wasn't the woman he wanted.

"That porch could use some paint. Actually, it looks like the boards are rotted. You could use a whole new porch." Donna stopped at the bottom of the stairs, her arm in the crook of his elbow, like it belonged there.

It didn't feel the slightest bit right. After last night, it felt especially wrong, although it wouldn't have felt right even without knowing how perfect Lark felt in his arms.

He didn't appreciate her assessment about his porch, either, as accurate as it was.

Lark dreamed of sitting on this porch. She didn't mention that it was old, somewhat dilapidated, needing at the very least a fresh coat of paint. Probably needing to be completely replaced as Donna said.

Lark was happy with it, as long as he was there.

But Lark couldn't become a veterinarian if she was sitting on his porch watching the sun go down every night. She couldn't live up to her potential and help the people that she was born to help, if he took her away from what she was born to do and kept her for himself.

She had her whole life stretching out in front of her, and he'd made a promise.

"That's the first thing you can do with my money. You can replace the porch."

Donna didn't know anything about dairy farming. There were a hundred other things he needed to do before he could replace the porch. Fixing the tractor was number one.

Then, he'd be too busy baling hay, chopping haylage, and putting it up to even think about the porch. Probably until October. If he was blessed to have a few extra weeks of an Indian summer, he might be able to get the porch done. After the harvest was in and everything was hunkered down and ready for winter.

He wouldn't be doing the porch one second before that.

Lark would understand.

Donna obviously didn't.

"Cat got your tongue? You haven't said much. You thinking fifty million isn't enough for you?"

"It's plenty."

Lark didn't care that he didn't talk either. Knew that sometimes it just took a little while to get himself collected.

He needed to stop thinking about her, stop comparing Donna to Lark. Of course Donna wasn't going to measure up.

"Listen, I don't want to waste my time. I don't have much left, and if you've decided it's a no, spit it out."

"I haven't decided that. I..." The words needed to come, he had to force them out, he had to say what needed to be said, in order to go forward. Donna wouldn't be alive long, and then he would wait until Lark was ready, wait until she graduated.

Maybe they could date the last few years of vet school. Maybe they could...spend holidays together, summers, something. Once Donna was gone, next year this time, he and Lark could be together again. Not together-together, but friends. Friends who spent time together. Friends who maybe even visited each other at college.

Although he was old enough to be a professor and wouldn't fit in with any of the kids, but Lark never cared.

"All right, just in case that was your answer, I had my lawyer draw up the prenup that I told you about. You can go ahead and read it." She walked toward the door, like she was expecting him to open it for her.

He put his hand on the doorknob and said, "If you don't mind, I'll sit out here."

"You go right ahead. I have myself all fixed up, because I figured once you sign the prenup in front of a notary, we could just go head down to the courthouse and get married. North Dakota doesn't have a waiting period, and I don't have much time. The sooner we get this marriage done and over with, the sooner I can tell my kids to buzz off. I just went ahead and put in the prenup that once you say 'I do,' twenty-five million dollars will be deposited in your account. My lawyer's taking care of it, but it should be in there next week this time."

She stopped talking, took a couple of breaths, the only sign that she was sick, and said, "It takes a little longer when you're dealing with those large sums of money."

The question he hadn't thought to ask swirled around in his mind. How long until she died? How did he know for sure that she was sick? With the way that she looked today, he wouldn't have guessed that she was sick with cancer, let alone dying.

How did a person ask someone if they were sure they were going to die and not sound like he was eager for the event to happen?

He kept his mouth closed, as he normally did, and took the folder she fished out of her purse. He opened the screen door for Donna to walk through, then he walked over to the swing, opened the folder, pulled the papers out, and started to read.

Chapter 24

Lark shook hands with the accountant who sat at the table, collecting money for the auction.

She'd just purchased a tractor, an old one, true, but one that Jeb would be able to work on easily with no problems.

One that ran, because she'd taken it for a test-drive.

She laughed, never thinking that she would test-drive a tractor nor buy one at an auction. It was true Jeb hadn't paid her much; she barely earned in a week what most people would earn in a day, and that was for working seven days a week, all day long, and sometimes eighteen hours a day in the summer.

She hadn't minded because she loved every second. She also saved almost everything he'd ever given her. And she had the money to buy the old tractor.

At least to be able to get his hay started, and then, if he was able to get his old tractor fixed, he might have two.

There were often fields they couldn't get to, and with two tractors, and both of them working as hard as they could, they could make twice as much hay.

She had so many hopes and plans and dreams, things she wanted to try, things she knew would help the farm, that she could hardly contain herself.

Then, as she was turning from the table where she'd just paid, she happened to see a little boy, a dog sitting at his feet, with a big box beside them.

Whimpering came from the box, and Lark walked over, taking a peek. The most adorable puppies, six of them, wiggled around inside of it.

The word FREE was written in big black marker on the side of the box, in a hand that looked like maybe his mom had helped him do it.

"Want a puppy, lady?" the kid said, making Lark smile.

"That's a nice dog you have there. That's the mom?"

The boy nodded his head proudly, putting a hand on the top of his faithful dog. "Someone dropped her off along our driveway when I's in kindergarten. She been with me ever since. She ain't never had no puppies before, but this year, she had twelve. I told Mom I could keep them all, and I'd get a job so I could pay to feed them, but Mom said twelve puppies was too many. I had to give them away." He looked forlorn. "So far, I've lost five, but I still have six more."

Lark's brows drew down. "But if you've given away five? And you still have six to go, that's only eleven," Lark said, not knowing why she was talking to the little boy. She did not need a puppy.

The boy looked both ways. "I kept my favorite one back."

"Oh, you did?" Lark said with her brows lifted.

The boy nodded his head. Then his face dropped. "I just wanted him to go to a farm. He's like his mom, and he can round up cows real good." His face brightened. "Spikey goes out with me every day to get the cows, and he's the only one of them pups what looks like he's gonna be like her."

"I see. So you're going to keep Spikey?" The farm could use a dog. Jeb could use, needed, a dog. It was high time he got one.

"Mom won't let me, but I didn't want just anyone to have him. I want him to go somewhere where he's going to be on a farm, not tied up in the backyard or stuck in a house all day long. He was born to run," the boy said proudly, sticking his chest out, like he was talking about himself and not the pup.

"I was thinking about getting a puppy for a friend of mine." Of course. Jeb loved Buster so much. He gave him such a great home. He would give Spikey one as well. She wasn't sure how long he would want to wait until they got married. She would do it today, but he would probably want a wedding just because he would think she wanted one. He might even insist on it. It could be Christmas before they had everything planned out. In the meantime, she wouldn't have to think of him being alone.

"Is he a farmer?" the boy asked, lifting his brows and looking eager.

"He sure is. Actually, I just bought that tractor right there for him. I was on my way to drive it out to him," Lark said.

Earlier that morning, while Jeb was milking, she'd had Charlie drive the four-wheeler out to the farm and she picked Charlie up in her car. She hadn't taken the time to say anything to Jeb, because she didn't want to spoil her surprise when she came driving down his lane in the tractor. She would assume that he would take her home, but sometimes he was busy, and she didn't want to keep him, if he had something he was working on.

Of course, she wouldn't mind the extra time with him. Maybe she wouldn't tell him that she had the four-wheeler parked in the shed and just let him take her home. For some reason, she wanted to spend every second she could with him; even if that meant an extra ten minutes in the car while he drove her home, she'd take them.

"So he wouldn't be stuck in the house all the time?" the boy said, and Lark had to remember that he was talking about the puppy.

"No. The last dog he had, Buster, followed him everywhere. Out to the barn to milk cows and out to the field to do hay. He liked riding in the tractor, and when he wasn't riding, he walked along behind. Just back and forth, across the field. All he wanted to do was be with Jeb."

"Really?" the kid said.

Lark nodded.

"Then maybe Jeb would take my puppy. He'd be a good farm dog."

"If you think so," Lark said, peering over the edge of the box at the swarming mass of puppies that had flopped on top of each other and now breathed in and out, little tails and feet twitching in dreams.

The boy looked both ways, and then he reached under the table and pulled out a little wiggling mass. It was spotted black, what Lark thought was probably parentage of a blue heeler back in the line somewhere, its ears floppy, its tongue sticking out, trying to lick the face of the boy as its paws all struggled together.

Beside the boy, the mama whimpered, which made the pup struggle even more.

"This is Spikey," the boy said, holding him up.

"And how much do you want for Spikey?" Lark asked, knowing the sign on the side of the box said free, but the boy was giving up the puppy that meant the world to his heart, and she didn't want to just take him.

"Mom told me I had to say they were free, because she didn't want me to bring any back home."

"Well, you need to get a little bit of money for a dog of that quality," Lark said, and she reached into her pocket for the twenty that she'd stuck in there earlier, thinking that she might buy Jeb and herself lunch if he showed up.

Of course he didn't, which she had expected. Crowds weren't his thing, and he would fix his old tractor before he bought anything else.

She straightened the bill out and held it out to the little boy.

"Is this enough?" she asked.

The boy looked at the money, his eyes bright.

"The whole thing?" he asked.

"Yeah. He's probably worth more than that, but that's all I have with me today," Lark said and shrugged her shoulders.

If she had a fifty, she would have given it to the kid. Just because she felt so bad for him at having to give his puppies away.

At least he kept the mom.

That wasn't enough money to get her fixed, but maybe his parents would come up with the rest. She kind of hoped so, but she didn't say anything. That wasn't her area.

The boy snuggled the puppy, and Lark's heart softened into a mushy pile of goo at the fact that the boy didn't grab the money but snuggled his puppy to say goodbye to him first.

That told her more than words how much the pup meant to him.

"Here," the boy said, and there were tears in his eyes as he held out his beloved dog.

Lark could hardly imagine trading money for an animal, but that's the way the world worked, so she held out her twenty and said, "Here."

She waited until the boy reached to take it before she took the wiggling mass of soft fur and wet tongue and flailing paws from him and cradled it next to her chest.

The pup wanted to sniff her all over and lick every part of her too, and she held him and petted him for just a bit.

"All right. Spikey is going home to be with Jeb and will keep Jeb company, since Jeb lives by himself. I think they're gonna really love each other."

The boy nodded, jerking his head up and doing a quick swipe at his cheek, before he shoved the money in his pocket and turned away, burying his head in the mama dog's neck.

Lark swallowed, then walked away, her heart breaking for the little boy, but part of it was smiling, too.

Jeb was going to love his puppy and his tractor, and while her gifts were nothing compared to the necklace that he'd given her the night before, or the kisses, or the way he'd made her heart sing, and her soul soar, and her whole being feel like she couldn't be loved any more than what he obviously loved her, at least it would be a little start.

Chapter 25

Lark hadn't stopped smiling, the whole time she drove out to Jeb's farm. The tractor worked like a dream, an old but solid piece of machinery, and the pup had settled down to sleep in the crook of her arm.

She was so happy to give someone she loved gifts. Some of her family had tried to talk her out of buying the tractor, telling her she was crazy, but they didn't understand. Jeb needed it, and she didn't need the money. It wasn't enough to pay for even one semester of school, and she didn't want that anyway. She wanted Jeb, and the farm, and the life that they would have together.

Smiling, because she knew that Jeb would see things her way, and eager to get out, eager to hold him again, eager to remind herself that last night wasn't a dream.

Kissing Jeb was the best thing that ever happened to her, made her feel warm and good the whole way down to her toes, but it also made her want more.

Maybe, if she got there early enough, they could spend some time kissing before milking time.

There was an odd car parked in front of the house when she got there, one she didn't recognize, but there was no one in sight, except Jeb, who sat on the porch swing, which was strange as well.

Normally in the middle of the day, he'd be doing something, mending fence, fixing a piece of machinery, taking care of animals, cleaning the freestalls, something.

There was a long list of things he could be doing, and he never sat around.

But there he was, on the porch swing and not looking very happy to see her.

He held some kind of folder and papers in his hand, and she wondered what in the world he could be looking at.

Maybe it was an itemization for the work that he needed to have done for the tractor.

That didn't make a whole lot of sense to her, but it was the only thing she could come up with unless the fancy car came with a fancy lawyer, but surely if that were the case, Jeb would have known it and told her last night.

Parking the tractor right beside the strange car in the driveway, she shut it off and jumped down.

By then, Jeb had come to the edge of the porch, standing at the top of the stairs, his arm on the banister.

Since the puppy was wiggling in her arms, she led with that.

"Look what I brought for you!" she said, holding the puppy up and getting ready to bound up the steps, but at the last second, the look on his face stopped her and she ended up standing at the bottom, looking up.

"What's wrong?" she asked, her stomach bobbing, fear squeezing her rib cage.

Why was she afraid? Why did she feel this odd, unbalanced feeling, like her world was about to be shifted in some major and catastrophic way?

"Lark, I need to talk to you."

Never good words. Especially when accompanied by a look like that.

But before she could say anything, a woman, with perfectly styled blonde hair and beautifully applied makeup, dressed in a classically flowered top and flowing pants, stepped out through the screen door, bracelets jangling on her wrist and rings glistening on her fingers, diamonds in her ears.

Lark tried to figure out how old she was, but she wasn't sure. Older than Jeb. But a lot older? In her forties? Jeb was thirty, so... Could the lady be forty? That wouldn't even be as big of an age gap as was between her and Jeb, twelve years.

But somehow the lady seemed so much older than Jeb, like they didn't belong together.

Didn't belong with her arm around him, her body pressing into his, her head leaning against his shoulder.

"And who is that, Jeb, my dear?" the lady said, making Lark's eyes widen and her foot take a step back.

"Jeb?" Her brows went down, and she felt like she was in an alternate reality. What was going on?

"Didn't you tell her about us?" the lady asked, sliding her cheek against Jeb's shoulder as she lifted her head and looked into his eyes.

Except he wasn't looking at her, he was staring at Lark.

Jeb wouldn't be able to find his words; he wouldn't be able to tell her what was going on. He'd need time to think.

"All right. Since Jeb doesn't want to tell you, I can. I'm sorry, the cat must have his tongue," the lady said, and she giggled a little, like that was somehow funny.

The cat didn't have Jeb's tongue; he just needed time, needed a minute to get his thoughts together. And then he would tell her. For some reason, she really wanted him to say whatever needed to be said, and not this woman who leaned into him like she owned him.

The way Lark had been leaning into him last night.

"Jeb and I are getting married. This afternoon." The lady tilted her head. "Aw. Poor little baby. You can't possibly be out of high school. You're way too young for Jeb." The lady tsked the way an adult did to a child who had done something really, really wrong.

"Looks to me like Jeb's marriage is a surprise to you. It didn't need to be. Jeb could have told you himself if he wanted you to know. He's been here all day. But we were just on our way out. In fact, I had just gone to freshen up, to make sure I look as good as I can, because I'm sure Jeb is going to want pictures to hang on the wall. I know I do. After all, when two people are married, they do love to have pictures taken together."

She looked over and blinked her eyes at Jeb. "Don't they, dear?"

Lark wasn't sure that she and Jeb ever had a picture taken of the two of them. In fact, she was sure they hadn't. She hadn't even considered taking one last night.

It made her sad, that they didn't have anything to remember the time they had by, and then it made her angry. Why did she want to remember it? He didn't just decide this morning that he was going to marry this woman. He had to have known last night.

Hadn't he?

She needed to know. Of all the things that were going through her head, that seemed to be the most important.

"Did you know this last night?" she asked, and she knew there was pain in her voice, a lot of pain, but she couldn't help it.

How could he have done this to her? How could he have bid on her meal? Danced with her? Held her in the moonlight, kissed her so sweetly, so passionately, so beautifully that she lay in bed with her fingers touching her lips for hours, thinking and smiling and dreaming.

How could he have done that to her knowing that he had...someone else?

Jeb jerked his head up and down; it wasn't a big gesture, and it didn't last long, but it was all she needed to know.

Last night when he had held her, kissed her, danced with her, he'd known that he was going to marry this woman today.

If hearts could explode, that's what Lark's chest felt like. Like bits and pieces of it went everywhere, except she didn't even think she had a heart in her chest. She had given it to Jeb.

This man, this man who could hold someone and make her feel precious and beautiful and cherished and plan to marry someone else the next day, wasn't the man she knew. Wasn't the man she'd worked with for years, wasn't the man she'd been in love with just as long.

"Jeb? This isn't like you at all."

Jeb shook his head, like her question didn't matter. Like he wasn't even going to answer it, like there wasn't an answer to it, and he wasn't even going to dignify her statement by arguing that it was, it was exactly like him, and her heart hurt so hard, her breath came in short gasps, her body felt cold and hot and weak and so exhausted she could barely stand and she didn't know what else to say.

And then the wiggling puppy reminded her that she came bearing gifts.

Was she going to take them back?

Just because Jeb wasn't the man she thought he was?

Jeb didn't lean into the woman, he didn't move to put his arm around her, he didn't lean his head down and breathe deeply, like he loved the air that was next to her, like he couldn't get close enough to her, like he wanted to be beside her for the rest of his life.

The way he'd acted with her last night. He wasn't doing that today. Not with this woman.

She couldn't figure out what she was missing. She had to be missing something.

"Are you really getting married today?" she asked, her words sounding weak, faint, like she was talking from a long ways away, through layers and layers of pain and heartache.

Again, that short jerk, his head going up and down, the only sign she had that it was true. It was all true.

She needed time to think, time to process, time to let the pain settle into something she could manage. She loved him. Just because he hurt her, because he'd done something so terrible to her she could hardly stand from the pain, just because he wasn't doing what she wanted, did that mean she didn't love him anymore? Was her love that fickle? Did it depend on the way he treated her? Wasn't love more than a feeling? More than words, more than kisses in the dark?

When she said she loved him, she didn't just mean she loved him as long as he did what she wanted him to do. That she'd be nice to him as long as he was nice to her.

She'd meant she loved him, Biblically loved him. Sure, the words were nice and the kisses rocked her world, but love was action, it was a choice she had made, and that choice didn't change just because her heart hurt and her mind couldn't grasp exactly what was happening.

If she loved Jeb, she loved him. End of story. And she would show him. But she couldn't stay, because that would be too painful.

She stepped forward.

"Well, then consider Spikey a wedding present." She wasn't quite sure where that came from. She didn't want to talk at all, was more than a little surprised she still could.

She didn't want to move forward, but she walked to the steps and set the puppy on the porch at his feet.

She knew he wanted one, knew he needed one, and guessed, especially if he was marrying this woman, for whatever reason, he would need one, because...he would still be lonely.

The woman didn't get him, didn't get him at all. Didn't understand the cat didn't take his tongue, didn't know that he loved sunsets and quietness and needed time to form his words before he spoke. That he wasn't a child, and wasn't stupid, and wasn't any of the things that the lady acted like he was.

He was everything Lark loved. And apparently, everything she couldn't have.

She took a breath, stepping back down off the porch, while the puppy whined at Jeb's feet. She had one more thing she needed to say.

"The tractor is yours, too. I bought it for you."

She looked at the woman, and just below the confident surface, she saw someone scared and alone, someone desperately trying to make the man beside her belong to her, when he really didn't.

Suddenly, Lark felt pity for her. Jeb would never love that woman the way he loved Lark. And that woman would never understand him, either. That was sad. To go through one's life and never know the love of a good man. And yeah, whatever Jeb's reasons were, why he had done what he did, she didn't doubt for one minute that he was a good man. In fact, if she had to guess, she would say that he would say he was doing what he was because he wanted the best for Lark.

She disagreed, but that didn't make him wrong. It didn't make her hurt any less, either.

She stepped up one step again and held her hand out. "I'm Lark. I used to work here."

And that was true. She hadn't planned the words until she said them, but of course she wouldn't work here anymore. She couldn't.

And that was almost as painful as knowing that she would never have Jeb. Almost. Well, not even close, but it still hurt. She'd miss milking cows and making hay on hot summer days, and the feeling of satisfaction after they'd spent all day working and knew that they were storing things up for the winter so they would survive for another year.

The woman looked at her hand, like she couldn't believe that Lark was holding it out.

Lark waited. Remembered the first time she'd held her hand out to Jeb, with one of those long silences where he needed to process things in his mind before he could make his tongue work and his body move.

This woman wasn't having that problem, and Lark wondered if maybe she would be cruelly turned away.

But the woman, bracelets jangling, held her hand out. Her rings flashed in the sunlight.

Her hand, when it gripped Lark's, was cold and dry, smooth, a sharp contrast to Lark's rough and calloused and chapped hands. Like the lady's hands had never touched a cow, never put a milker on, never washed an udder. Never drove the tractor, never lifted a hay bale, never fed a newborn calf. They were soft, inside hands.

Maybe that's what Jeb wanted. A soft woman, with soft hands, pretty sparkly jewelry, and perfect hair.

That had been her last night. Maybe that's what had attracted Jeb all of the sudden. She hadn't thought of that. That he had resisted her for years, then last night, he'd kissed her over and over again.

He'd given her jewelry too. Her hand went to her neck, where the lark necklace he'd given her hung. She touched it; part of her wanted to rip it off and throw it at his feet, and part of her wanted to cherish it forever.

She would probably not do either, and she dropped her hand. Not wanting to destroy something so beautiful, to inflict pain just because she was hurting.

She swallowed. And turned.

"Lark. Wait."

She didn't remember walking to the shed, didn't remember getting on the four-wheeler, starting it, pulling out.

She did remember looking over at the porch. Jeb stood ten yards away from it, the puppy in his arms, standing behind the woman's car, like he had wanted to come over and talk to her, but she left too fast.

She supposed the time for talking was over. She would have thought she would never have said that, but it was true. The time for talking was over.

Chapter 26

J eb stood in the driveway, watching Lark leave.

He knew this was going to happen, knew it was going to hurt both of them, but he hadn't had any conception of how much.

He wanted to drop to his knees, curl in on the pain. He'd never had anything that felt half as bad as this.

But instead, he couldn't help but watch Lark until she faded off in the distance, and even then, he watched the dust raised by her machine, like focusing on her would keep him from doubling over, fading into nothing but pain and heartache that lasted forever.

The puppy in his arms whined, and he stroked the fur absently.

She'd known exactly what he needed, exactly what would work for him, and she got him the best two things in the world she possibly could have. A tractor to get his hay in, and a companion to...not replace her but help soothe the ache, the sharp, almost unbearable pain, that her absence caused.

"Who was that?" Donna said from the porch.

He stood for a few more minutes, not wanting to turn around and talk to her, knowing there were some things he needed to say.

He turned around, finally, swallowing hard.

How did he describe Lark to Donna?

"She's the best person I know. She...was a lot nicer to me than I deserved." An understatement. She should have shot him. But of course she wouldn't. He'd counted on her kindness for him to be able to keep his word. He hadn't even realized how much. "She knows me better than anyone."

"Oh. I thought she was your girlfriend, then she said she worked here, but she doesn't look like a farmhand."

No. She didn't. She was too small, too fresh faced, too innocent and pure. He didn't know what she looked like. An angel, maybe.

"All right. Are you ready to go? I'd rather take a nap, but we need to get to the courthouse before it closes, and we need to get these papers notarized first. Did you have any questions?"

"No. You were fair." The papers said exactly what she said they were going to, down to the twenty-five million that was supposed to land in his account sometime next week.

The last thing he wanted to do was get in his truck and marry this woman, but it was like he'd told Lark, sometimes life didn't go the way a person wanted.

He found a bowl of water for his pup, Spikey, she said his name was, and a box to keep him in while he was gone. He'd have to dig all of Buster's stuff out when they got home. He didn't move the tractor, didn't have time to go do any hay today. It would be there tomorrow.

They went to the notary, had the papers notarized, had a short and impersonal ceremony in front of the magistrate at the courthouse.

Jeb hadn't thought about rings, and he wouldn't wear one anyway. There was too much chance it'd get caught on something and take his finger off. Donna already had three rings on her left ring finger, and there wasn't any room for one of his anyway, even if he did give her anything that looked even remotely as nice as what she was already wearing.

She talked, but not like Lark did. Not silly things, fun things, happy things, or farm things. She'd spent her time trying to make him smile.

Donna got annoyed with him both on the way there, and on the way back, and while they were waiting, because he didn't answer fast enough.

He was used to that, people wanting him to speak faster, or speak at all, and him not being able to.

He figured Donna would get used to it too.

Lark had known and handled it in such a way that made him feel like she understood him.

He figured Donna would never do that.

After their marriage, Donna had to run into the restroom at the courthouse, and Jeb walked outside, pulling the cell phone out of his pocket.

He had an idea that had been stirring in his head, and he wanted to take care of it immediately.

He dialed a number he hadn't ever dialed before but had gotten one day long ago and had kept, because he figured he might need it sometime. Not like this, never like this, but sometimes life threw curveballs.

The phone rang in his ear three times before Clay Stryker's voice sounded on the other end.

"Hello?"

"It's Jeb."

"Jeb." Clay seemed to take a deep breath, maybe a second one. Then he said, "You kept your word."

"Yeah."

"I know I should thank you, but I'm not sure I can right now. I've never seen Lark like this."

That didn't make him feel any better. In fact, it made him feel worse. "She told me she didn't have enough money to go to school."

"I'll take care of it," Clay said.

"No. I will." Jeb didn't give him any time or room for argument or discussion. He was going to take care of it, and that was final.

Clay didn't say anything.

Jeb took a few minutes to gather his thoughts, and then he said, "I don't want her to know. I'm going to send the money to you, you tell me how much. You make sure she gets it. Make sure it goes to college. Make sure she has everything she needs, and if there's ever anything that she needs that what I send doesn't cover, let me know." It was the least the man could do. After the sacrifice he'd required of Jeb, and after Jeb had given every single thing that he'd asked, both of them wanting the very, very best for Lark, Clay had better not deny him this request. Which was more of a demand.

"You got it, man."

Jeb took a breath, then another one, and then he said, in a more humble tone, "Thank you."

"Jeb?"

"Yeah?" he said shortly.

"It should be me thanking you." A pause. "I think."

Jeb grunted, but he didn't say anything. He felt like the world should be thanking him, felt like the sacrifice was too big.

"Jeb?"

Jeb grunted again.

"Would you like to write to her?"

"No. She won't write to me anyway." She'd probably never talk to him again. He deserved her hatred. Deserved her scorn. If she was hurting anything close to what he was, he wouldn't blame her if she came back out to the farm and beat him over the head with a pitchfork.

"Write her as her anonymous benefactor. Send your letter to me. I'll make sure she gets it. If she wants to write back, I'll make sure you get hers."

That was far, far more than he thought Clay would do. He hadn't really thought Clay even approved of him or liked him at all. And yet now he was giving Jeb a lifeline. Something he could do so that he wasn't completely cut out of her life. He had the opportunity, if he played his cards right, if he could get the words to come, to know what was going on in her life.

There was no way he was going to pass this up.

"I'll take you up on that." Not telling Clay what he'd done felt like lying. "But you should know something first." He didn't want to say that, but he knew he needed to.

"What?"

"I got married today."

Clay was silent for a moment, and then he said, "It had to do with money, didn't it?"

Jeb had no idea how Clay knew that. But he did. And Jeb could no more lie to Clay than he could fail to keep his word. "Yeah."

Clay sighed, a long, deep, drawn-out sigh that tore at Jeb's soul, like Clay had wanted something else for him, and now, whatever it was, whatever hopes he'd had were dashed into a million tiny pieces, and he was mourning their loss.

"That reeks, man." Another long sigh. "I'm sorry."

"Me too." There wasn't anything else to say. It was true, he was sorry. Sorry he got married, sorry he couldn't have Lark, sorry that life sucked sometimes.

"I'll make sure you have my address. But I understand if your wife doesn't want you to write."

"I'll see what she says," Jeb said, even though he wanted to say, *it's not love, I don't owe her anything, I can write to whomever I want to.*

That was not true. He'd pledged his life and his love to the woman in the bathroom at the courthouse, to Donna, to someone he barely knew and wasn't even sure he liked, let alone loved. But he had to keep the vows. Still, there was nothing wrong with writing to someone as a benefactor, corresponding and finding out how his money was being used.

He would present it to Donna like that, and he didn't think she'd have a problem with it. After all, she didn't love him any more than he loved her.

"Thanks for calling."

"Yeah. Take care." That's all he could say. He wanted to say, *tell her I love her, tell her I'll do anything for her, tell her if she ever needs anything, all she has to do is say so. Tell her I'm stupid and wish I wouldn't have done what I did.*

But it really wasn't true. Because, although he hurt himself and he figured he'd hurt her worse than anybody had hurt her in her entire life before, if he had to do it all again, he would.

He didn't deserve someone like Lark, and he wished he could go the whole way back to the day she'd asked for a job and he could just tell her no.

It would save them all the pain.

He hadn't moved from where he stood, still thinking, when Donna came out of the bathroom.

She looked tired, like she actually had cancer. When she hadn't before.

"I'm tired. Let's go home," she said, leaning into him and walking to the door.

He would need to go grocery shopping at some point, and maybe they'd figure out what their jobs were going to be. But maybe not. Maybe he was just supposed to take care of her.

He wasn't sure and didn't have the brainpower to figure it out. Just knew when they got home, he'd get his dog and get the work done that needed to be done. And if he had more work to do, he'd do it. Because that's what he did.

Chapter 27

Dear Benefactor,

Wow. I can't believe that someone that I don't know, or maybe someone I do know, has just given me money for college. It's amazing to me that someone even knew I might want to go or that I had even applied.
I don't know. I'm just feeling very mixed up right now, even though I've settled into my classes here in Florida, and I'm enjoying them for the most part. I've made some friends, but I'm still homesick at night. For the most part during the day, I can stay busy and not think about it.
Anyway, I wanted you to know that your money is going to good use. I'm studying hard, and I've gotten perfect scores on every test I've taken so far. I'm sure that's probably not the way my college career is going to go completely, but I appreciate your sacrifice, and I don't want to take it for granted.
Maybe you don't know that I wasn't even sure that I wanted to go to college. I'm still not sure I want to be here, but I certainly am not going to waste the opportunity or the money.
My brother Clay suggested that you might want to know what's happening with the person that you're sponsor-

ing, and he suggested I write a letter.

I suppose he's probably right; it will keep me accountable, even if you're not interested. He said that if I sent the letter to him, maybe you'd write back.

I'd really like you to. I'd like to find out who you are. I'd like to be able to thank you in person. In particular for giving me some direction in my life at a time when I really felt like I had no direction. Actually, I felt like I didn't want to go in any direction.

I've never understood anyone who would say that they felt like they want to die, but that's the truth with me. I wanted to die.

Anyway, that part is over, the hard part from what everyone says, and now, although I don't have the innocence that I used to, and I don't quite have the zest for life I'd had forever, I do have the drive to do the best I can because someone believed in me.

Of course, I've had someone who believed me before, and then...they let me down.

I suppose that's why it's important that I find my worth in Christ. At least that's what that part of my life taught me anyway. That I can't depend on people, can't depend on how I feel with those people or how they make me feel. I have to depend on Jesus. Because humans are not infallible, and sometimes they mess up. Sometimes they hurt you, and if that's where all your worth is, you land pretty hard.

Anyway, I'm rebuilding and trying to remember that Jesus is my foundation. Hopefully I built a little smarter this time. I guess that's what hardships do to you, right? They make you smarter.

Anyway, I hope I don't get bitter and mean. I've always wanted to be happy, kind to people, and the kind of

person who makes other people smile, not the kind of person that people groan and want to run from when they show up. That's pretty much how I feel right now.
But day by day, I'm doing just a little better.
Anyway, that's my life so far, and I hope to hear from you.
Thanks again.

Yours truly,
Lark

Dear Lark,

I was very happy to get your letter. I definitely would like to hear what's going on with you. I knew you were a good "investment," and I know that you'll take the money that you're using and use it to make your life a blessing to others.
I think you're right about rebuilding with your focus on Jesus. I suppose I know a little bit about that too.
Regardless, I'm busy, and I'm not much for writing, but I'm not too busy to read your letters, please keep them coming.

Sincerely,
Your benefactor

Dear Benefactor,

First of all, thanks for writing back. I don't have a problem chattering, but it's nice to know that my chattering is going somewhere. It's perfectly fine if you don't write back a lot. I understand. You're the one who's spending money on me, and you want to know that money is going to good use. You probably don't have much to tell me, although anything you want to tell me about yourself, you're certainly welcome to. I've been told I'm a good listener, but I'm probably better at talking.
It seems like people like me, people who don't have a problem talking, are drawn to people who don't talk as much.
I've spent some time thinking about that, although that's probably all I better say about it.
I've been in my Bible more, and I have to say, I can feel the growth almost. Feel my spiritual life strengthening, my relationship with Jesus becoming more important to me, stronger, more of an anchor for my soul. I understand that a lot better now than I used to.

Funny, because I'm only eighteen.

I suppose I was young and naïve. I feel like I'm old now, but I'm sure I seem young to you.

Anyway, I almost didn't come to school. I suppose you might as well know that.

I had been given an offer, in the form of a letter, shortly after everything went south in my life. In fact, I believe it was two days later, if I recall correctly, although everything for weeks after that day seems so black to me.

Anyway, the letter said I would inherit one billion dollars upon my marriage, as long as I stayed in North Dakota with my husband.

Which, of course, I had no desire to leave North Dakota. So that wasn't a big deal.

The big deal was, the only man I wanted to marry just got married to someone else.

So I burned the letter.

Anyway, I'm here at school now, thanks to you. And thanks to you again, I'm rebuilding my life. This time, the foundation is solid.

I still haven't missed any questions on any test, although I did miss one on a quiz. I'm taking biology, and it was a lab. I was supposed to differentiate between two different nerves, and I mixed them up. Although, I have to say, I'm not sure that the professor knew exactly which ones they were. But we have to take his word for it, don't we?

Anyway, I'm enjoying my classes, and much to my classmates' dismay, I spend most of my spare time studying.

I also have a job. I know, I know, you pay for everything. Clay explained it to me, but I want to feel useful. So, I'm walking dogs. And I'm volunteering at the Humane Society. I clean out cages. Which, I have to admit, isn't that fun, except for the time I get to spend playing with

the dogs while they're out of their cages.
I don't get paid for that, but I love it.
Anyway, that's all that's going on for me. Is there any-
thing you can tell me about yourself?

Sincerely,
Lark

Chapter 28

J eb sat at the kitchen table, Spikey at his feet. Donna had long since retired for the night. Treatments were hard on her, but the doctors had said that the cancer was shrinking.

They called it a miracle. They hadn't thought that it was curable, but the last hope they had, the last experimental chemo they tried, was working.

Jeb was happy for Donna, but he found it hard to be happy for himself.

Donna was nice in her own way, but after being with Lark, no one would ever compare.

Trying not to think about it, he looked again at the letter in his hand. She'd been offered one billion dollars if she married.

There he was, only offered twenty-five million, and he'd jumped all over it like a fly on honey.

Lark had burned her letter.

He squeezed his eyes shut, trying to push back against the pain that seemed to lurk constantly in his chest.

Where his heart used to be. Hearing that, knowing that they could have gotten married, and while money didn't solve all of the problems, it would have helped a lot. It was hard to swallow.

But it didn't change the fact that he'd made a promise to Clay.

He supposed he could sit on his integrity, knowing he did the right thing, keeping his word, wondering why God had made the timing the way He had. But integrity was a cold bedfellow.

Dear Lark,

I was speechless when you told me about the letter you received. One billion dollars is a lot of money. Far more than I have.
I... I guess I'm glad you burned it. It might have been tempting for you to marry anyone, just to inherit. I certainly couldn't fault you for that.

Jeb had done it. But he could hardly say that in his letter. He thought over the words in his head before he started writing again.

I think you made the wise choice. I suppose I've seen people who say they marry for love, and then they fall out of love, or whatever. I think that the best relationships are relationships with a solid foundation. And the foundation that you were talking about, Jesus, is probably the best foundation that a relationship could have.
I suppose you've inspired me to work on that myself. I always try to read my Bible, but I've become much more meticulous about making it a daily habit. Actually, as the nights get longer, and the days get shorter, and my work hours ease, I've been doing it in the morning and the evening.
Thanks for the push. I needed it, and I appreciate it.

Sincerely,
Your benefactor

Chapter 29

Lark walked down the sidewalk of her college campus, unable to believe that she was actually graduating from that school. Seven years of study, hard work, and dedication was now paying off, and this was quite possibly the last time she would ever set foot on this campus again.

She would miss it, but she was ready to go home. Home to North Dakota. To the land of her heart.

Seven years had made the ache in her chest less. She didn't hurt quite so bad when she thought of North Dakota and home. She could actually think of Sweet Water without thinking of a herd of Holstein cows and the farmer who cared for them.

She had heard that farmer had gotten married just like that woman had said he was going to.

She'd heard he was still married, and that didn't surprise her. He'd be married until one of them died. That was the way he was.

At least, the man she knew. He'd shocked her when she had found out that he was holding her while planning to marry another all along. That wasn't the man she knew, but she didn't think that the person that she'd come to know through all the years she worked with him had somehow morphed into someone different.

Over the years of her schooling, she'd realized that sometimes, people did things that were unexpected, and often they had what they felt were really good reasons for the things that they did.

That was probably what happened with her farmer.

It was easier for her if she didn't think his name.

Still, her family had made it down for her graduation, and she was especially happy to see her mom and her sister Charlie. Her brothers, Clay, Boone, Mav, Mack, Cord, all of them, had come, because they were proud of her. They wanted to see her. They wanted to celebrate her victory, but before she did that, before she walked across the stage, she had someone she needed to thank.

So, she went to her favorite place on campus, a bench by a weeping willow tree next to a small lake, where ducks and geese swam in tranquility, pulled a notebook out of her backpack, and sat down on the bench with her pencil.

Dear Benny,

Goodness, it seems like I know you so well by now. Seven years of writing. Seven years of working. Seven years of midnight panics, your words of assurance and comfort and encouragement. I don't think I would have made it through school without you. Actually, I wouldn't be here without you. You know that.
You feel like a friend. A good friend.
I suppose, since we send our letters to Clay, it won't matter to you if I move again, but I just wanted to say a huge thank you. Thank you for believing in me, thank you for supporting me, thank you for coming along during the time in my life when I really needed someone who thought I was more than what I thought I was.
That was you.
So, I know you're not here today, but I wish you would be. I wish you'd tell me who you were so I could thank you in person. But I understand if you still don't want to. Regardless, I was hoping you would continue to write. I can't imagine going through the rest of my life and never

talking to you again. Like I said, you've become a friend, a better friend than any I've made in school.

I'm planning on moving back to my hometown of Sweet Water, North Dakota. You probably never heard of it, because nobody has ever heard of Sweet Water, North Dakota. But that's where my heart is, and that's where I'm going to set up my practice. I decided that I wasn't going to work for someone else, but I was going to start my own and just see what the Lord did.

Who knows, maybe there'll be more than animals in my life.

Lark sat on the bench and put the eraser end of the pencil in her mouth, chewing on it lightly.

She wished she could talk Benny into telling her who he really was. She wished she could meet him. She wished she had a way of thanking him better.

But she was older now, and wiser, and she knew that life didn't always give a person the answers they wanted.

Sometimes they didn't get answers at all.

And that was when she needed to hold tight to God's hand.

Because God had never let her down.

That was probably her biggest takeaway from college. It was assuredly the most important one. She felt like college had given her grounding and a direction for her life, but God had given her purpose. Whatever He wanted, she felt like her life was His to use. He'd had to put her through a really hard time, bring her to her knees, before she was willing to give Him everything.

Looking back, she wouldn't want to go through it all again, but she was grateful for the experience.

If she had married her farmer and settled down on the farm, maybe she would have learned that lesson. Maybe there would have been money issues and hard times, and maybe she would have had to cling to God to get them through, but she kind of thought that she wouldn't have learned the lessons quite as well as she did because of the direction her life had gone.

She had to admit, she knew that God had been in control, and He had orchestrated it to be the very best for her that it could possibly be.

She certainly could not complain.

So, since I'm heading home, I was thinking about buying a small farm. I wanted to have Highlanders on my farm. They're such a fun cow, all shaggy with big, long horns, and great, gentle personalities. They are all the rage everywhere, but probably because they're all the rage, they're also extremely expensive. I'm not going to get one, even if I could afford it. Too much money. But I can look at them and love them, right?

I'm smiling now, because one of my friends, Jenny, told me that in her town in Arkansas, they have a mascot. It's a goat. Apparently, nobody knows who owns the goat, but it goes around, and everybody feeds it. It has a little shed to live in during the winter.

One day, the goat headbutted someone who was visiting the town. That person landed in a flower bed, and one of the town's residents, a young lady, helped the gentleman out of the flower bed, and apparently they fell in love.

Now, the town bills their goat as Cupid, the Love Goat. Wouldn't it be cool if Sweet Water had a mascot like that? I thought so after she said that. Actually, I was with a group of girls, and after Jenny got done telling her story, Riley said that in her Louisiana town, they have an alligator as a mascot.

But she made sure to let everyone know that the alligator was not a matchmaking alligator, and while people talked about alligator sightings, they certainly didn't get married because of it.
Every town has their quirks, I guess.
Anyway, I wanted to write one last letter out to you to thank you for everything and to let you know that should you ever want to, I'm available. I would love to meet you.

Love,
Lark

Chapter 30

J eb sat holding the last letter from Lark in his hand.

Donna had defied expectations and not only lived longer than what the doctors had given her but had been declared completely cancer free.

Seven years had gone by, and Donna was healthier than ever. She had a nutritionist and a chef, and they cooked her the healthiest meals from organic food, using all the latest research of health and nutrition to make sure that her cancer didn't come back.

She'd long since moved away. His farm was way too far out for Donna to be happy, once she figured out she wasn't dying.

She'd given him a line about loving the farm when she wanted him to marry her, but that was just a line. Sweet talk, to get him to do what she wanted.

She did it a lot. Like he couldn't see right through what she was doing, telling him what she thought he wanted to hear so that he would do whatever she wanted, give her what she wanted, be agreeable.

Not that there was much she ever asked for. Not since she'd moved away. But when she wanted something, she felt like she needed to butter him up. It annoyed him, but he never told her he could see what she was doing. It was just the way she was, he supposed.

Spikey whined at his feet as he pushed the swing with one foot, the other leg stretched out across it and one arm stretched out over the back.

For most of the last seven years, he'd been alone.

Except for Spikey. Spikey had become attached to him and never left his side.

It was like Lark had known. Had known he would need a friend, a companion, something to help fill the hole she left behind.

He lived for the days when he got her letters, and she always wrote at least once a week. Sometimes twice, depending on what she was going through, and he always answered the night after he got it, giving himself a day to think about it, especially if she was asking for his advice.

A few times over the years, he'd asked Clay for advice on what to say to her.

Clay never said anything, not about Donna, not about his marriage, not about the letters they sent.

Whether Clay read them, or whether he didn't, Jeb didn't know, and he supposed he didn't care. He never said anything inappropriate. Lark didn't know who he was, and as far as he was concerned, she would never find out.

He didn't want the letters to stop. And Clay had never said that they had to quit. So, as long as Clay was willing to send letters between them, and as long as Lark was willing to write, Jeb was going to see if they could still stay in touch.

I was hoping that we could continue to write. After all, the money I gave you for college will pay returns for the rest of your life. I'd love to see how far it goes. But, not just that, I want you to know that Clay will still have money available to finance you. So, if you want to build a herd of Highland cows, go for it. If you want to buy a farm in Sweet Water, Clay will have all the money you need. Just tell him how much. Money doesn't have to be something that you ever worry about. Do you understand that?

Your letters are the bright spot in my day. I hope they don't stop, but I understand if you find other things to interest you.
I definitely welcome them and will continue to respond as long as you write.

Sincerely,
Your Benny

Chapter 31

Lark sat down at her desk at the farm she bought in Sweet Water several years ago.

It was dark, late, and the girls who stayed at her house were sleeping.

Somehow, she'd started taking in teen girls who needed a change of scenery, needed to get out of a bad situation, needed to turn their lives around.

She hadn't been sure exactly how this started, although she supposed a couple of her friends from college had maybe started it when they'd asked her if she had room or knew someone.

She hadn't realized it, but her reputation had been of being wise and honest and insightful. Apparently, some of her friends had figured that she would make a good mom.

She wasn't quite sure whether that was true or not, but whether it was, she had ended up with girls she couldn't imagine living without.

Still, they kept her busy, along with her vet practice, and helping Mabel, who was an up-and-coming vet. She was still in school, although now, years after she had started school, classes could be done online for a lot of it. That's what Mabel was doing, and helping out.

Lark loved her, appreciated the company, and appreciated the help even more.

But whatever she was doing, she would never be too busy to write to Benny. She gave him all the credit for turning her life around, him and God.

God first, of course.

She smiled, clearly being able to see God's hand in her life now. Where, as an eighteen-year-old, she just couldn't. Couldn't imagine that there could be anything more than a farm and cows and the boy she loved. Man. He had been a man then, and he was a middle-aged man now.

She wasn't quite sure what he thought of her, since she hadn't seen him in years. He didn't call her when he needed a vet for his cows, even though she'd taken over the practice of the old vet, Dr. Ringwald, who had retired shortly after she graduated from vet school and came back to Sweet Water.

True to his word, Benny had given her the money for a farm, and while she had waffled back and forth, she'd finally taken it, glad she had, because then she had a place for the girls.

She'd been able to start her practice, and she was debt-free, unlike a lot of people who had to start in life with a lot of payments to make before they could start earning money for themselves.

It was a hard life. She worked a lot, sometimes more than she thought she could, but she felt like she was doing good in the world.

Although, she felt like if she had married her farmer, her life would still be happy, she would still be enjoying it, but she knew God's way was best.

Picking up a pencil, she started to write.

Dear Benny,

We got a new girl today. Another one. I told you I wasn't quite sure how this was all happening, but I guess God knows. I certainly don't think I'm qualified to be a moth-

> *er, but the first couple of girls that we've had have been here for a while, and they seem to be completely turned around.*
>
> *I suppose you know that this would never have happened without you. I don't know where you are, what you're doing, but I will be eternally grateful for the difference that you've made in my life.*

Lark lifted her pen for a moment. She always wondered what would have happened if Jeb would have agreed to marry her.

None of these things would have happened if she had been with him. She wanted to hate him, wanted to at least dislike him, and think about all of the things that he had kept from happening in her life, but the reality was, because he walked away from her, he allowed all of these things to happen. He was the catalyst for everything. Benny might have financed it, but nothing would have happened if Jeb wouldn't have said that she needed to go to college and become a vet.

Still, after all these years, it hurt to think that he could have walked away from her so easily, gotten married the next day, and she never heard another word from him.

She wished she could put that out of her mind, but it was impossible.

Maybe she just needed more time. Although, it had been more than a decade.

Apparently, when she fell in love, she fell for a lifetime.

Lord. I'd like to get married. I'd like to have children. Of my own. Like to have a home and family. But if this is what You have for me, a thriving practice and a home for girls, please help me to be satisfied and not long to have a lifetime love that only happens between a man and woman.

Writing to Benny often made her stop and pray. She thought of things she didn't normally when she had a letter going to him.

And of course, I can't say that without thanking you for the money that you sent over the years as well. I know I thank you over and over, for everything, but I don't want you to think that I am not appreciative of each individual thing that you do. And, as always, I'd love to meet you if you ever allow it. So I can thank you in person.

He'd always ignored her requests to meet, and she supposed that that was just as well. After all this time, she wasn't sure whether she actually wanted to meet or not. Of course, on the one hand, she wanted to be able to thank him in person, but on the other, he might be disappointed in her. Although, she'd always considered the possibility that her benefactor was someone she knew.

Back when Clay had first told her about her benefactor and about the money, he said that the man had wanted to remain anonymous.

After that, Lark had never asked, because she didn't want to tempt Clay to betray a confidence.

She continued on with the news of her farm and her veterinary practice and told the story of a couple of cute antics that the girls did. And then she said,

I don't know if you remember, but a few years ago, as I was graduating from college, I told you about a goat that was a mascot in Arkansas and about a Louisiana town that had an alligator.
I had talked about getting Highlanders and I'd also talked about having a mascot for Sweet Water, but I hadn't really connected the two of them.

Man, sometimes the Lord works in mysterious ways, because our town actually has a Highland steer as a mascot! Can you believe it?
I certainly couldn't. It's crazy to me, the idea that Sweet Water has our own mascot. And it's a Highland steer.
I smile every time I drive into town and see him.
There actually have been some reports that he's a match-making steer, although I can hardly believe that. But I suppose stranger things have happened.
Anyway, I thought you'd get a kick out of that, and I just wanted to let you know, because we'd talked about it.
Kinda funny when you think about it.
Thanks again.

Love,
Lark

Chapter 32

Jeb sat on the tractor, not even moving from the mailbox, while he tore open Lark's letter.

He read it as fast as he could, just to get all the information in one big gulp, and then he went back and read it more slowly two more times.

His grin got bigger each time.

She'd heard about Billy. That's what the townspeople had named the steer that he'd gotten and released in town.

Jeb had bought him and brought him into Sweet Water on a dark night with no moon. He'd given Billy a big pile of hay and a scoop of grain to tide him over until the town woke up.

They were taking care of him just like he thought they would, and from what he heard, Lark had even been called out to check on the steer several times.

He smiled to himself. The matchmaking qualities of the steer had been proclaimed far and wide, and tourists were actually coming to Sweet Water to see him.

He couldn't have planned it better, doing down to the letter what Lark had asked for.

She hadn't asked him to do anything. It was just a dream of hers, and...it wasn't exactly his mission in life to make her dreams come true, but if there was something she wanted, and it was in the realm of possibility, he would make sure it happened.

"She likes him, old Spikey." He scratched his dog's head.

Spikey had gone from an energetic young pup, to a middle-aged, looking very hard at old age, companion and friend.

Lark's last gift to him. He still admired what an amazing person she was to have set the dog on the porch, instead of carrying him away with her.

She had given him everything she intended, even though he'd given her nothing but pain and heartache in return.

And Spikey had blessed him over and over and over again in the years since.

Still smiling, he chugged down the driveway. Sometimes after he was done with the farmwork for the day, after he'd gone out and gotten the mail, and gone back to the house, the idea of it waiting for him, empty and silent, felt like a weight in his soul, depressing and hard. But it never felt that way after he got a letter from Lark.

He would smile for days after reading her letter. They always thrilled him, although they were bittersweet in a way.

After all, she wasn't that far from him now.

It had been hard the first year or so after she'd moved back. He'd known she was just across the prairie, and he'd wanted hard and long to go to her. Sometimes at night, he'd lie in bed and think about her, the breeze blowing across first her house, then his. So close, and yet there was a huge chasm between them that could not be breached.

He hadn't expected Donna to live as long as she had, and even though she didn't live with him, even though he barely talked to her, he couldn't not keep his vow.

As though thinking about Donna had conjured her up, his phone rang.

He dug it from his pocket, seeing it was Donna's number, and he swiped and put it to his ear.

"Hello?"

She usually called when she wanted something. Sometimes it was a water leak in her house that needed to be fixed, a lightbulb she needed changed, furniture moved, and several times, her yard maintenance man hadn't shown up, and she wanted him to come mow the grass.

She lived two hours away, but he tried to do what she asked, because as her husband, he felt like it was his responsibility. That's what she was to him—a responsibility. Although, she had deserted him, technically, and didn't live with him.

He'd gotten the porch fixed before she moved out, but he'd never bothered with anything else, and the only thing he had used her money for was to finish paying off the farm, to buy a new tractor, and to do whatever Lark needed.

"Jeb. It's Donna, your wife."

"Yeah?"

Interesting. She was emphasizing that she was his wife. Like he didn't know. He knew. *He knew.*

"I'm moving back in."

"Okay." He had never asked her to move out. She had bought a place closer to Fargo, bigger, closer to town, more convenient, and then she began to spend more and more time there, until when they'd been married a year, she hadn't lived with him at all anymore.

It really hadn't made much difference to him. In fact, he supposed if someone pressed him, he'd have to admit he liked it better when she wasn't there. Even if the house was big and empty.

"Don't you want to know why?"

It couldn't be because Lark was back. She'd been back for years. Five at least. Maybe more. He tried not to count.

"Why?" he said, figuring that's what she wanted him to ask.

"I just got back from my doctor's visit today, my cancer is back."

He swallowed. "That's hard."

She must have been devastated. They had celebrated when the cancer had shrunk, and shrunk again, and shrunk some more.

About the time she wasn't living with him anymore, they found out that the cancer was completely gone.

Of course, it took five years for her to be declared cancer free, and as far as he knew, she hadn't had any trouble with it since.

Now...

"I want to move in with you. I don't want to be alone. I'm scared."

He didn't know what to do when she started crying on the other end of the line. "Last time they figured out something that would work. They'll do it again."

"I might die! I don't want to die!"

He thought about the conversation he had, years and years ago, with Lark. Talking about death, and how it just inspired a person to live better. About dying well, about using one's life to prepare to have a courageous death.

Maybe they had been big words. The older he got, the more he wasn't sure he wanted to face death. It was a scary thing. Dying.

"I'll come out and get you. You won't be alone." That was the whole reason they'd gotten married in the first place. He'd support her, take care of her, help her however he could. It's what he agreed to. Just because the timeline wasn't what he'd been told it would be didn't give him the right to not do what he said.

"No. I want my car while I'm there."

"I'll make sure things are ready for you."

"Jeb?" Her voice had lowered, and she said his name softly.

"Yeah?"

"You never expected me to live this long. I... I always wondered if you regretted... There was that girl." She took a breath, then blew it out. "But you kept your word. I... I wondered if you would."

He had. He'd kept his word to Clay. And he kept his word to Donna. The vows that he had made to her. After all, what kind of man would he be if he only kept his word when it was easy? And the kind of man he was was because of Christ.

Maybe his logic was a little convoluted, but if he kept his word, it was because of God, not because of Jeb.

"I'll keep my word. You can count on it." He hadn't wanted to. It would hurt Donna if he admitted exactly how much he hadn't wanted to, but he had.

"All right." She took a shaky breath. "I'll see you in the morning."

"I'll be ready for you."

They hung up, and he sat on the porch step with his dog, forearm on his leg as dusk slowly faded into deep night, but still he sat there.

Donna trusted him. She came back when she was sick. She knew he'd take care of her. She thanked him for keeping his word.

And yet just across the prairie, less than ten miles away, his heart beat inside the chest of a different woman.

Still, he'd take on and fight this round of cancer, do his very best to make sure she survived, even though it wasn't what he wanted, because her death would set him free.

As far as he knew, from the letters she'd sent, Lark had never even looked at another man.

He fingered the letter he still held in his hand. She had never even mentioned anyone. As far as he knew, he'd been the only one.

That made him sad in a way. She had so much to give. She would have made some man an amazing wife, but she used her life wisely instead, doing so many good things for so many other people, and he couldn't be more proud of her.

He wanted to be the kind of man who deserved a woman like that. Even if he never had her, he wanted to be the kind of man who deserved her.

On that thought, he scratched Spikey's ears, stood, thought about all the things that were going to need to be done the next day, and turned his mind to getting ready to fight cancer, again. And he walked slowly into the house, thinking that sometimes a man's integrity was a cold bedfellow.

Chapter 33

Five years later...

Dear Lark,

I've decided that I'd like to meet you. Are you still interested?

Sincerely,
Your Benny

Dear Benny,

Yes! Just tell me where and when.

Love,
Lark

Dear Lark,

I'd like to meet at the white church in Sweet Water. The old one. Out back, at the bench under the big oak tree at five o'clock on Friday. You won't have time to write me back, so I'll just be there, and if you can't make it, we'll set up a different time.

Love,
Your Benny

Chapter 34

"**N**o, you take it over there, that garbage can needs to be emptied. Be sure you don't spill anything when you take it out," Lark commanded, sending Heavenne toward an overflowing trash can.

"You look exhausted, honey." Her mother came up, putting an arm around her.

"It's been quite a day. I think all of Sweet Water decided that the funeral was a good time to get together and celebrate."

"You know how small towns are, we never pass up an opportunity to turn something into a festival."

She smiled at her mom and nodded. That was absolutely true.

"You said you had an appointment, and I don't want you to be late. So you go ahead and go."

Lark nodded. Her appointment was at the old church, the one that she'd gone to as a girl.

They built this newer, bigger church, further outside of town, but they still used the small white church that was beside the community center for get-togethers and that type of thing.

She swallowed. "I feel like maybe I should get dressed up. I corresponded with this man for years, and now I'm finally going to get to meet him."

Her mom smiled, and then to her surprise, her mom put an arm around her and pulled her into a hug. "You are one of the most beautiful, kind, considerate, and forgiving women I know. I hope this meeting turns out to be the very best thing that ever happened to you."

Those seemed like odd words, but she hugged her mom back and said, "I just know that it's going to be that important. I... I just want to thank him in person. He's made such a difference in my life."

"It's funny how sometimes in order to do our very best, for ourselves, for someone else, we have to step back."

Those seemed like odd words too, but then her mom pushed away and smiled at her.

"God rewards the faithful. Sometimes we have to wait for those rewards, but they come. I used to think that God never gave me what I wanted, only what I needed, but you know, sometimes He gives us what we want too." Her mom smiled, and to Lark's surprise, there were tears in her eyes.

"Mom? Are you okay?"

"It's almost five o'clock, and if you're going to be there on time, you need to get going."

Lark knew she was right, but a lot of people were heading out and she'd seen Jeb outside not that long ago. She didn't want to run into him. She managed to be in the kitchen when he went through the line, and she hadn't needed to say a word to him. Even though the dark blue shirt he was wearing made his eyes as blue as the September sky and he looked older, sad, silent, and serious, and like the Jeb she'd known and loved, and she wanted to go out and put her arms around him. She didn't even need to say anything.

She chuckled. Maybe she'd grown up some.

Except she hadn't, if she was still wishing that she could be with Jeb.

On the day his wife was buried no less. What kind of person was she?

Regardless, she slipped away, walking down the sidewalk, stopping to scratch Billy's ears as he stood on the sidewalk, almost as though he'd been waiting for her. She'd seen him often over the years, being called to check him when someone in town was sure something was wrong with him.

Typically it turned out that the only thing wrong with Billy was he was trying to get two people who belonged together forever together.

"Billy, I really think you are a matchmaking steer."

Billy pushed her a little with his nose, almost as though telling her that she needed to get moving. She was going to be late. She could see the church just ahead and a little bit of the cemetery, although the rest was hidden by the buildings in front.

"All right. I'm going."

But as she started to walk, Billy fell into step beside her.

Odd.

But she didn't need a human to talk to, and when she was nervous, she talked a lot more than she typically did, so she said, "What is he going to think of me? Do you think he's going to look at me and wish I would have turned out differently? That his money was wasted?"

Billy didn't answer her, of course, just kept walking toward the church.

"I probably could have done a lot more with it. A lot more with myself. After all, Sweet Water is just a small town. I could have been somewhere in a big city making all kinds of waves."

She'd never felt driven to be anywhere but where she was. In fact, she'd always been pretty content wherever she was, whether it was in college in Florida, or vet school in Oklahoma, or wherever she landed, she was just pretty happy.

Although there was always a hole in her heart.

"I guess there always will be too," she said to Billy. "It's too bad you couldn't match me, but I think I'd be immune to anyone but Jeb. Even after all this time. I...saw him today, and...all I wanted to do was walk over."

She couldn't say any more. Some things just couldn't be spoken aloud. Even to a steer.

She walked past the last building and turned up the alley next to the church. She could see the oak tree and the bench. The sight sent a pang through her because of the memories they held and how the sight brought those memories to the fore.

There was a man standing behind the bench, perpendicular to it, with his hip leaning against the back, his head turned toward the street, as though he were watching for her.

He was tall and dark with a slightly pouchy stomach, and he had on the same color of blue shirt Jeb had worn for the funeral.

Somehow she thought Benny would wear a business suit, but this man had on jeans, one booted foot propped up on the back of the bench.

He leaned on his leg, but when he saw her coming, his foot dropped to the ground, and he straightened.

His cowboy hat was pulled low over his eyes, and all she could see from that distance was a square jaw, a day's growth of stubble, hands that looked like a working man's hands, and shoulders that were broad, like they could carry the weight of the world.

She reached for the gate, grasping the latch and pulling. It squeaked just like it had that night so long ago.

Interesting that Benny would pick here. He didn't know the history. She never told him, although it wasn't quite the right time of day. The sun was sinking low in the sky, but there was no sunset, no stars, no moon, no night breeze.

Still, the quietness of the cemetery was the same. It brought back memories of their conversation about death that she'd never quite forgotten. It had shaped her life probably more than any other conversation she'd ever had.

Maybe someday she'd be able to stand in front of Jeb as an adult and not want to revert back to the teenage girl she used to be, throwing herself in his arms, forgetting about using words, and just kissing him.

She closed the gate and started up the hill, lifting her eyes and getting a good look at Benny as he reached up and took off his hat, throwing it on the bench.

Her heart twisted. She looked, then looked again. Benny looked an awful lot like Jeb. She wouldn't know that, if she hadn't just been to Jeb's wife's funeral and just seen Jeb standing at the casket. Same shirt, same short hair, same...blue eyes. She was fifteen feet away when she realized it *was* Jeb.

She froze. Part of her wanted to run, although she couldn't figure out which way. Back? Away? Toward him? Just run and throw her arms around him?

It took her brain a few moments to process, to understand, to see what was right in front of her.

Jeb had to be Benny. Her benefactor. The man who had sponsored her, but it couldn't be, because Jeb was a farmer, a poor, struggling, North Dakota farmer, not a millionaire who sponsored teen girls as they went to college and vet school. In fact, half the time she was gone, she expected to hear Jeb had lost his farm.

"You?" she said, only realizing then that her hand had landed on her throat. "You're Benny?" She shook her head, like it couldn't be. There was no way.

But it was Jeb, no doubt. He stood there, staring at her, not saying anything. She realized there were tears flowing down her cheeks, but she smiled anyway. So much like Jeb.

"Woman. You always rendered me speechless."

She laughed. She hadn't rendered him anything. That was just the way he was.

"I'll wait," she said, shaking her head, still not understanding, figuring she could wait while he found his words.

"Wait here?" He opened his arms.

Maybe her heart beat once, maybe twice, before her feet were running and she was the little girl she didn't want to be throwing herself into his arms, wrapping them around him, and holding tight, pressing her wet face against his shirt and breathing deep of hard work and character and fresh air, feeling the solid man under her, and never wanting to let him go.

She didn't care what he said. Didn't care if he hurt her once. Jeb was here, and he wanted her. She wanted him, and of course, they were completely different people now. Their lives were half-lived, maybe even more, but it didn't matter. Because they were together.

"I missed you. I missed you so much," he whispered into her hair, his mouth beside her ear, his lips at her temple, his arms pressing her close as he laid his cheek on top of her head, easing his desperate grip on her, like he was deliberately letting her breathe.

But she didn't want to breathe, she just wanted to be as close as she could to the man she'd...loved for her entire life.

"How? How are you Benny?"

"The night before the auction, Donna offered me fifty million dollars to marry her."

She gasped. Part of her was outraged, but before she could say anything, Jeb continued.

"She told me she had terminal cancer and just wanted to get married so her kids couldn't stick her in a nursing home. I knew you needed to go to college, to become a vet, that we would be separated for seven years, and if I did what she asked, I would have the money to finance you, since you had just told me that you didn't have the money for college."

"Oh... Jeb. I can't... You didn't."

She pressed her lips against his neck. He'd married Donna so he could send her to school.

And then she realized something. Jeb knew everything. She'd written to him at least one letter a week, usually two, for the entire seventeen years they'd been apart, and she hadn't even known it.

"You know everything about me, and I know nothing about you."

"Shhh. I'll tell you anything you want to know. But the most important thing is that I love you. Next, I still have Spikey. Next, I still get up in the morning, work on the farm, milk cows, and in the evening, I go to bed thinking about you. Dreaming about you. Wishing you were there."

"Donna?"

"It was a business arrangement. A platonic marriage. All she wanted was a buffer between her and her kids and to not be sent to a nursing home, to have someone to care for her. I promised her that much, then she miraculously got better and stayed better. But she didn't want to live on the farm, so by the time we were married for a year, she moved out. I spent most of the last seventeen years alone...with just my memories of you. And the letters you sent. They were lifesavers to me."

"You're talking. How are you talking this much!" She couldn't help it, she was laughing and crying and doing all the things, feeling all the things, wanting to be all the things.

"It's you. Because of you."

"We could have gotten married. You didn't have to marry her."

"I promised your brother. The night in the loft when you and I were looking for the kittens, when he talked to me. I promised I would help you become a vet. I wouldn't stand in your way. He wanted me to promise, so I did. Because I always wanted the best for you."

"You did. You did."

She couldn't say that maybe the best for her was to be with him, whether it was, whether it was or wasn't, they were together now, and to fuss about water under the bridge was a waste of time.

"Marry me?" he said next to her ear. "I know you deserve a better proposal, flowers and candy and lights and all of the pretty things, but I want you. I've wanted you for seventeen years, more, longer, back when you were too young for me to even think about, I wanted you. Will you? Marry me?"

"Yes. Yes. If you hadn't just asked, I was getting ready to ask you myself. I'm done waiting. Done wasting time that I can spend with you."

"We're both done."

"Tomorrow?" she asked.

"Tomorrow. Tonight. Right now. I don't care. As long as it involves you being with me and us never being separated again."

Then she thought about the girls she had, her vet practice, her farm, her life, everything.

"How are we going to figure things out? They're more complicated now than they used to be."

"Sell my farm and live on yours. Sell yours and live on mine. Your girls are our girls. As long as I'm with you, even if that's in a tent on your bedroom floor, I don't care. Whatever it takes for us to be together. If you'll still have me."

"Of course I'll have you. That's ridiculous. I never stopped wanting you. Never."

She pulled back enough so that she could look into his eyes and smile in his face, but she didn't quite get that far, because as she pulled back, he moved closer, and her arms slipped around his neck, and she went up on her tiptoes as he lowered his head, and she would always claim forever after that it was her who kissed him, but he would say he kissed her, and she supposed it didn't really matter, because the breeze and the tree and the quietness and reminder of the preciousness of life of the cemetery and the feel of the strong man before her, so different than the young man he'd been seventeen years earlier, but still the same. Still the same character, still the same integrity, and all the better, all the sweeter for the years that passed between, and it didn't matter. She kissed him with her whole heart and soul, kissed him with the knowledge that this time, he said yes.

Epilogue

E zra Thatcher stood in the back of the church and watched as Sweet Water's veterinarian married her lifetime love.

He couldn't imagine a woman being faithful to a man for twenty years, especially when the man wasn't doing anything to keep her happy or whatever else it was that women thought men should do on a daily basis or they got angry and irrational and stormed out of their marriage.

He shoved a hand in his pocket and tried to control his thoughts.

Not all women were like that. There were women in the world like Lark. Women of character who kept their promises and didn't think that equality meant that women got everything and men got nothing and that was fair and right.

Of course, he didn't know many women like that. His sisters, maybe. And Lark. And he wasn't even sure about Lark, since he didn't know her that well, just knew what the town said about her.

Outside the church window he could see Billy wandering slowly up the alley beside the church. The ladies needed to be careful or the steer was going to upset all their carefully prepared tables of food.

He slipped out of the back as the preacher declared them husband and wife and Jeb bent his head to kiss his smiling bride. He didn't really want to watch that anyway. Not that he wasn't happy for them, he was, but it just made it even more crystal clear how lonely his own life was and how hopeless he felt about doing anything about it.

Even if he wanted to, he needed to adjust his attitude about women. They weren't all like his ex. Surely.

As he walked around the church, he saw a group of kids playing tag, all dressed up in their Sunday best while Alice, his sister's best friend, watched them.

Ha. She wasn't watching them, she was playing with them. As short as she was, and with her hair flying and her laughter trailing over the warm summer air, she just looked like one of them.

Alice had lost her parents when she was young, and had spent more time with the Thatcher family than she had with the aunt who had taken her in. She was almost like a sister to him, except, she wasn't.

His siblings had whispered over the years that she had a crush on him, but he'd brushed it off as an infatuation, knowing he wanted someone who was more his age, more mature and sophisticated, someone who challenged him intellectually and had things in common with him and not a woman-child that ran around playing tag and would be windblown and dirty as they lined up for lunch.

Alice grabbed a little boy as he squealed and laughed, twirled him around and set him down, running away laughing while he chased her. She ran around the swingset where another little boy jumped on the fellow chasing her, and she pulled up, laughing.

Her laughter faded as her eyes moved across the parking lot, maybe seeing that the guests now spilled out the back doors, and she paused, her eyes widening and her mouth opening as she caught him staring at him.

He turned his head quickly and strode to the food tables, glancing over them as though checking to see that everything was in order. A mistake, because Mrs. Turner grabbed his hand and slapped a ladle in it, telling him he could fill up juice cups.

It was something to do, which was probably better than standing around with his hands in his pockets. Weddings weren't his thing and the sooner he could get back to the ranch and up on his horse, the happier he'd be.

Alice's laughter floated across the breeze and he had the thought that maybe that wasn't entirely true. He pushed it aside and focused on the drinks. He wasn't interested in his sister's best friend.

Thanks so much for reading! If you'd like to read more from Jessie Gussman, check out the first book in her reader-favorite Blueberry Beach series, *Yesterday's Treasures*.

Enjoy this preview of *Yesterday's Treasures*, just for you!

Yesterday's Treasures

Chapter 1

This is the letter that Adam Coates found sitting on his kitchen counter the day his wife left him:

Dear Adam,

I'm sorry this is going to come as a shock to you. I've tried to figure out how to tell you, and I just haven't been able to.

I want you to know, first of all, that I admire your dedication to your job and the business that you've built, and that you get up every morning and you work hard. But I guess what you don't see is it was a single-minded dedication, and you've neglected your family in order to be a success.

I know I should have said something sooner, and the fault is mostly mine, except you are never here.

I didn't feel like this was a conversation we should have through texts.

You don't know it, because you haven't been around, but I was laid off from my job six weeks ago.

Maybe you don't remember, but I used to talk to you all the time about how much time you spent at your job and how I felt alone and neglected.

We didn't fight. I just tried to talk to you, and you would tell me that I was being dramatic or that it was what you needed to do in order to be successful and didn't I want you to be successful?

So yes, of course I did. So when I asked you to go get ice cream with me and you told me to do it by myself, when I asked you if we could have a date night and you said you were too busy, when I asked you to mark on your calendar Sierra's field trip but you couldn't because you were already planning to go somewhere else for your business, when I asked if we could take a weekend away and you didn't have time...when you forgot my birthday, when our 20-year anniversary came and went and you never said a word, when you took me out the last time and spent the entire time we were in the restaurant on the phone with one of your business associates...I didn't say anything.

I guess I'm saying something now.

I'm moving into the beach house. I'm taking Sierra with me. I've already withdrawn her from school here in Pennsylvania and enrolled her at Blueberry Beach High. I guess I would have told you I was doing that if you had been here.

I'm not angry, and I don't hate you, and I hope you don't hate me, but I'm tired of being alone. Tired of being a single mom. Tired of being married and washing your clothes and doing your shopping and cooking your meals and raising your child, and yet I don't have a friend or companion or someone to talk to or even someone to help me change a freaking lightbulb.

I'm not asking for a divorce. I'm just moving to our beach house, and I'll figure out what to do with my life there. I would have talked to you about that too, if you had been

here.
Of course, I understand if you don't want me and find
another woman to neglect. I won't fight it.
I'd thank you for the twenty years together, but it's been
more like fifteen years alone.
I wish you the very best.

Sincerely,
Your wife,
Lindy

Yesterday's Treasures

Chapter 2

Lindy drove toward their beach house outside of Blueberry Beach. Her daughter, Sierra, sat on the seat beside her. Sierra had headphones in, her cell phone in her hand, her thumbs running over it, and her feet propped on the dash.

A typical sixteen-year-old, and maybe a little bit belligerent because she had to leave the high school that she loved and start a new life somewhere else.

Just because her mother had decided to.

It had only taken eight hours to get here from their home just north of Pittsburgh, but she had to wait until Adam left for work at six o'clock before she could pull out.

After Adam left, she had to wake Sierra.

Adam hadn't even noticed that she'd packed her stuff.

He didn't come home until late, and he left early.

His business was doing fantastically well. They were making money and had been for years. Of course, when he'd just started, they'd had lean years. Everyone did.

When he first started out, she helped him with his books and took all the phone calls. Even with the baby crawling around, it wasn't hard. And Lindy loved it. Adam and she talked all the time about their plans and their dreams and their hopes for the business and family. It had finally gotten off the ground, and he moved to an office location where they had storage space as well as room for more employees.

She hadn't made the move with him because Lindy had been starting kindergarten, and it was only half a day. Someone had to be home in order to get her off the bus. Someone had to be home to put her on, since Adam left for work hours before the bus arrived.

She admired his hard work and his determination to succeed. Still did.

It was a crowded market, but superior service would always draw customers, and Adam provided superior service.

He also provided well for them, once the business finally took off about five years ago. For a decade, they didn't draw much of a salary and barely had enough to pay the mortgage and buy groceries.

She'd always been able to squeeze out the light bill as well, but for a long time, they were a one-car family.

Lindy didn't mind, except that meant, of course, that she couldn't go to work with Adam since she had to wait to put Sierra on the bus. He didn't have time to run her back and forth, and he needed their one vehicle for his job anyway.

It was fine, except it was the beginning of the end.

She parked their car, a nice, almost-new SUV, in front of their cottage on the eastern shore of Lake Michigan and pressed the ignition off, keeping her hands on the wheel, staring at the house, and blowing out a breath.

This was the beginning of the rest of her life.

Beside her, Sierra's thumbs moved rapidly over her phone and Lindy wasn't even sure she'd noticed they'd arrived.

The house was boarded up for winter. The planters that she'd had sitting on each side of the walk had blown over. There was some debris in the yard, and one of the shutters hung crookedly down, held by a single screw.

The house looked neglected.

She felt like she could relate.

She didn't expect to be coddled in her marriage, but there wasn't really a point of having a marriage when she did everything alone.

This wasn't her walking out on her marriage, exactly. It was more like her giving up.

She'd tried to gently nudge Adam, to mention that she wanted to do more than just sleep together for six hours at night.

And the man worked hard. She had to give him that. She admired hard work.

But wasn't a married couple supposed to talk occasionally?

Weren't they supposed to do things together once in a while?

Weren't they supposed to have some kind of shared time somewhere?

She tried to quit questioning herself and focus on what she was going to do.

She and Sierra would settle in here, and she would see if there was a job or something she could get in the town of Blueberry Beach.

She had skills. She'd been managing a candy store for years since working her way up from starting behind the counter when Adam and she had bought a second vehicle.

Her job in Adam's company had long been taken over by someone else, and he didn't even suggest that she work with him.

One more thing she'd gone out and done by herself.

Managing a candy store couldn't be too much different than managing some other kind of store, and she wasn't afraid to start at the ground and build up.

To start with, all she needed was money for groceries and electricity since the property was paid for as well as her car.

For the last five years, Adam's business had done really well, and she didn't want for anything material.

She just wanted a husband.

Maybe it was natural to feel like since he never spent any time with her, never wanted to do anything with her, he didn't really want her.

That he didn't like her. And if she believed in falling in and out of love, she would say he'd fallen out of it.

But she was more of the mind that love was an action verb.

An action verb she'd tried to live out for the last fifteen years, despite the fact that she saw less and less of the man she was trying to live the verb out on.

How do you show love to someone who doesn't seem to want to have anything to do with you? How do you show love to someone you never see? How do you show love to a man who is never around?

She blew out one more breath, and although she knew she probably wouldn't be able to stop herself from looking behind occasionally, she really wanted to focus on keeping her eyes looking ahead.

She prayed for guidance. Although she definitely did not have a peace about this decision, she'd also had doors open in a miraculous way. At least getting Sierra taken out of school and put in Blueberry Beach High.

It just so happened that one of her friends had moved here not that long ago.

Coincidence?

Maybe Lindy was just trying to grasp at straws to get God's blessing on what she knew she shouldn't be doing.

She should stay with her husband no matter how alone she was.

But things worked out with Sierra, and although her daughter wasn't super thrilled about the move, she wasn't fighting her either.

Sierra's feet smacked to the floor as she cracked her gum and blew a bubble.

Lindy tapped her on the arm. "Take your earphones off for a minute."

Sierra straightened, slipped her feet into the flip-flops she wore despite the cool spring day, and tilted her head, pulling one piece of plastic away from her ear. "What?" she asked, not unkindly but in a tone that let Lindy know she was being annoying.

"I want you to help me carry our stuff in, and there will be some cleaning that we need to do."

"I have to go to school tomorrow. I want to spend the day relaxing."

"You can relax after the work is done."

"I'm glad you brought me along. That way you didn't lose your slave."

It was borderline rebellious, but Lindy let it go, because she had brought Sierra along when Sierra would have been much happier living in a single-parent home north of Pittsburgh rather than living in a single-parent home in Blueberry Beach, Michigan.

She got the keys out of the cup holder and opened her car door. The last thing she needed to do was lock her keys in the car on her first night in town.

She supposed that would be a way to meet people, but not the way she wanted to.

She'd be handling everything by herself.

Not that she hadn't handled the mundane as well as emergencies by herself for years, but there was always that peace of mind in the back of her head that Adam could help her if she needed it.

That peace of mind was gone.

It probably had been a fantasy most of the time she'd cherished it anyway.

She shoved her phone in her back pocket. It contained the code to her car, which she could use to unlock it in case she actually did lock the keys in the car or lose them, but she wanted to be extra careful.

Shoving her keys in her front pocket after tapping the button to open the trunk, she walked to the back.

Sierra started grabbing stuff immediately, but Lindy just stood and looked at it.

She hadn't brought any furniture. The beach house had its own. Not super fantastic stuff, but stuff that would do.

She'd never needed fancy.

And she certainly wasn't going to start now.

Pick up your copy of *Yesterday's Treasures* by Jessie Gussman today!

A Gift from Jessie

View this code through your smart phone camera to be taken to a page where you can download a FREE ebook when you sign up to get updates from Jessie Gussman! Find out why people say, "Jessie's is the only newsletter I open and read" and "You make my day brighter. Love, love, love reading your newsletters. I don't know where you find time to write books. You are so busy living life. A true blessing." and "I know from now on that I can't be drinking my morning coffee while reading your newsletter – I laughed so hard I sprayed it out all over the table!"

Claim your free book from Jessie!

Escape to more faith-filled romance series by Jessie Gussman!

The Complete Sweet Water, North Dakota Reading Order:

Series One: Sweet Water Ranch Western Cowboy Romance (11 book series)

Series Two: Coming Home to North Dakota (12 book series)

Series Three: Flyboys of Sweet Briar Ranch in North Dakota (13 book series)

Series Four: Sweet View Ranch Western Cowboy Romance (10 book series)

Spinoffs and More! Additional Series You'll Love:

Jessie's First Series: Sweet Haven Farm (4 book series)

Small-Town Romance: The Baxter Boys (5 book series)

Bad-Boy Sweet Romance: Richmond Rebels Sweet Romance (3 book series)

Sweet Water Spinoff: Cowboy Crossing (9 book series)

Holiday Romance: Cowboy Mountain Christmas (6 book series)

Small Town Romantic Comedy: Good Grief, Idaho (5 book series)

True Stories from Jessie's Farm: Stories from Jessie Gussman's Newsletter (3 book series)

Reader-Favorite! Sweet Beach Romance: Blueberry Beach (8 book series)

Cowboy Mountain Christmas Spinoff: A Heartland Cowboy Christmas (9 book series)

Blueberry Beach Spinoff: Strawberry Sands (10 book series)